YOU'LL KNOW WHEN YOU GET THERE

You'll Know When You Get There

by

Lynda E. Rucker

Swan River Press
Dublin, Ireland
MMXXI

You'll Know When You Get There
by Lynda E. Rucker

Published by
Swan River Press
Dublin, Ireland
in October MMXXI

www.swanriverpress.ie
brian@swanriverpress.ie

Cover design by Meggan Kehrli
from "Olive Trees" (2015)
by Tobia Makover.

Typeset in Garamond by Ken Mackenzie

ISBN 978-1-78380-755-0

Swan River Press published
a limited hardback edition of
You'll Know When You Get There
in August 2016.

Contents

Haunting Places, Haunted People

The appeal of the haunted house story is widespread and runs deep; likewise, the feeling (it might be going too far to call it *belief*) that certain places are doomed, dangerous in some inexplicable, metaphysical way. And yet, for all their potential danger, haunted structures will always be alluring to some (you know who you are), as attractive as any bad boy, dangerous man, or *femme fatale*. We have relationships with places, too.

> *Carcosa is a sprawling heap of a house. It is the house of my bookish childhood fantasies. You know the sort. Old, and rambling, and surely possessed of hidden doors and passageways, and gruesome secrets.* (from "The Queen in the Yellow Wallpaper")

Our homes are vitally important; we could not live without them. Whether rented, inherited, or purchased through a lifetime of self-sacrifice and indentured servitude; whether we have built our dream home, or dwell, unhappily, in grim and unloved lodgings, the walls that surround us are a carapace, an exo-skeleton, just one step beyond our flesh and bones. Are we our bodies, or are we somehow distinct from them, as religions usually claim? Am "I" a spirit only temporarily inhabiting this form, before moving on, like the resident of a house? Or is even attempting to believe in such a split an indicator of madness? Where haunting is concerned, thoughts of madness inevitably creep in. In dreams, the house may stand in for the body—or one's life, anyway. (Surely the dream of discovering a previously unknown room in your familiar house is not about finding a new body part.) The house as much as the body is where we live; much like our relationship with our own flesh, we may feel comfortable, at one, or at war with it.

> *The heart of the house is beating. She can hear it, vessels in the walls, the walls that exhale with that life's breath that is just as sweet to the house's groaning floorboards and arched doorways and soaring cupolas as her own breath is to her; she can hear it, heart beating and moaning and sighing and "settling".* (from "The House on Cobb Street")

Lynda E. Rucker writes haunted house stories the way they should be written—hers are original, weird, and compelling, and as much about the people as the place. Not all of the stories in this, her second short story collection, are about houses, but every one of them hinges on the importance of the relationship between a particular person and a real place. It may be the American South, rural Ireland, urban England, or Portland, Oregon—wherever it is, you know, by the specificity and particularity of the descriptions, that the author is very familiar with the place she writes about. Her characters likewise seem real and non-generic; they are individuals with believable personal reasons for the situations they occupy. There is nothing random about the connection between person and place in these stories; here you will find no clichéd happy middle-class couples who *just happened* to buy a house where horrible crimes were committed and who are too dim-witted or stubborn to leave when they learn the ghastly truth (which of course has nothing to do with them). Instead, in Lynda's stories, unhappy people seek happiness, try to right old wrongs, are trapped by their background or family situation, romance goes sour, or—in this striking observation from "The House on Cobb Street"—in the same way couples remain unhappily stuck in a toxic relationship, "You entered into an abusive relationship with a haunted house."

It is the conjunction of believable characters and real places, convincingly depicted, that gives these stories their emotional power and makes the strangest of events seem almost inevitable. Lynda E. Rucker writes stories set in our own, recognisable, contemporary world, but she is also working in the classic tradition of M.R. James, Robert W. Chambers, Charlotte Perkins Gilman, Oliver Onions, Edith Wharton, etc. Two of the stories included here wear their influences on their sleeves, flagged up in their titles—yet "Who Is This Who Is Coming?" about an American fan's pilgrimage to the sites of some of James's most terrifying stories, or the brilliant "The Queen in the Yellow Wallpaper" which puts the iconic works of Robert W. Chambers and Charlotte Perkins Gilman with a hefty slug of contemporary gender politics into the blender, are much more than the sum of their parts; far from mere pastiche, they are new and powerfully memorable horror stories for our time.

No one who loves a good ghost story (and, really, who doesn't?) should miss the chance to read this great new addition to the literary ghost story tradition.

Lisa Tuttle
Scotland
June 2016

You'll Know When You Get There

For my mother,
Carolyn Nance Rucker

The Receiver of Tales

A letter arrives in the mail. That in itself is unusual enough. She had not realised people wrote letters any longer. She had not imagined anyone wrote anything any longer; isn't everything now encrypted in bits and bytes, nebulous as the spoken word? Schrödinger's writing; does it even exist if it isn't printed? She has never owned a personal computer, won't touch the things outside of work where she has to, can't abide them. First the future and now the present are passing her by. She is a thing of the past, and she knows it.

The envelope, dull and plain and white, tapped through the mail slot of the front door of the house she lives in, bears no identifying marks; its stamp is uncancelled.

She waits until she is back in her apartment to open the letter with trepidation and unfold the single sheet inside, upon which is scrawled in an unknown hand a single word: "Soon".

The world reels about her.

She is sick of all the stories she has to tell.

Not all of them are tragic, although the tales people feel compelled to share during the dark nights of their souls tend to have elements that are not the most uplifting. It isn't the substance of the stories, though, but the act of hearing them

3

and writing them down that has grown tiresome. She feels like the Ancient Mariner, clawing at wedding guests and rambling on about an albatross, only she is begging others for their stories, not telling them herself.

Afterward, she writes them down and now her fingers are permanently ink-stained. Ruben's fingers had looked like that as well, she recalls; only paint—instead of ink-stained. She has to tell herself he'd not known what he was doing when he pushed the painting under the door of her little studio apartment in the old Victorian, where only a thin wall divided her place from his. The painting had made a scraping noise across her floor, and she'd jumped up, opened the door and looked down the long hallway and seen no one.

"Who's the girl that listens to the Pixies all the time?" said the attached note. It hurt to remember Ruben, and she hadn't listened to the Pixies in twenty-five years.

"I'm Aisha. The Pixies girl," she said to him the next day, her knuckles dropping away from the door because he answered it before she could knock. In her other hand she held the painting, swirls of doomsday oranges and red, a dying sun obliterating a blistering landscape. Ruben waved it away.

"It was a gift," he said. "Keep it." His eyes were red and moist. She thought he looked like someone who had not slept for a very long time.

Is this the story I'm writing now? Aisha asks herself. If so, this is a wonder indeed. What happens when the storyteller tells her own story? Doesn't it stand to reason that this will be the last one? What a blessing that would be, if she still believed in blessings. And the story surges out of her.

This was Ruben: a shock of dark hair (she'd always thought he looked like Nick Cave), an incessant parade of identical black T-shirts, the smell of cigarettes (unfiltered Lucky Strikes), a voice that sounded too deep to belong to the weedy boy in possession of it, and paint spatters, everywhere, on his forearms, his rumpled jeans, even on the rough hardwood floor of his apartment. "You'll have to pay for that when you move out," she said, and he just shrugged.

The old house off Boulevard had been chopped into six tiny apartments decades earlier: all day and all night long you heard your neighbours walking, arguing, fucking, sobbing, cooking, watching television. It was a shocking kind of intimacy, if you thought about it: Aisha, who had grown up with two sisters and two brothers, had nonetheless never experienced less privacy. Ruben dug it. He would lie for hours, he said, one ear to the floor, absorbing the lives that echoed beneath him. At first she didn't believe him—who would—but later that would be the least of the difficult things to believe. But she had to believe all of it. By then she'd seen—no, heard—too much.

"Aisha," he said. "What kind of name is that? I've never heard it before."

"I don't know. It was the name of my mom's best friend, but she died when my mom was pregnant with me. So I was named after her." Even before birth, someone else's past had claimed her.

"Oh." Ruben regarded her with those steady grey eyes. "That's wild."

He said it so softly, and she couldn't figure out what he meant by it. What would be wild about it? Later she would wonder whether his ever-abstract way of speaking was something he possessed before or if the vagueness had come upon him over time as it had with her. Sometimes she saw herself as others must see her, a frizzy-haired woman of indeterminate age, arms and legs covered on even the hottest day, speaking in a voice so soft it barely rose above a whisper with words that escaped her so often she would sometimes stand silent for minutes at a time. Nothing, she had learned over what seemed like an endless lifetime, made people quite so uncomfortable as a stretch of silence, particularly when you stood in front of them and presented them with that silence.

Uncomfortable at first, at least. Before long, they would be telling her their darkest, most painful secrets, the things they tried most to keep hidden away from the people who loved them, the stories that poisoned their lives if they allowed themselves to think of them at all.

She still lives in the chopped-up house on Boulevard. Over more than twenty years she has scratched and scrawled words on every surface from floor to ceiling. She dwells in a palace of ink. Words upon words and stories upon stories. She will not do as Ruben did; she will not weaken; she will not take the easy way out; she will not infect others as he infected her.

Ruben had tried to paint the virus out of himself but it got him in the end. She will never forget the sight of his body swinging in the incongruous sunlight that spilled through the window of his apartment. She stood aghast in his doorway for what seemed like hours. She did not scream or cry. She took in the swirling dust motes, the bluebottle fly dashing itself against the window, the heat of the room and the smell that had brought her to use the key he'd entrusted her with. It was summer. A perfect summer's day. In her nightmares it is always summer.

She burns the envelope and the paper that came with it in the enamelled bathroom sink. The flames, flaring briefly, scorched the word that appeared there. Later she stands naked and shivering under the jets of hot water from the shower. She had to give up lovers long ago, when she began carving the stories into her flesh. Beautiful expanses of scar tissue cover her arms and legs, her stomach, her breasts, the tops of her feet.

She isn't Ruben. She won't weaken like he did. Ruben had been too afraid of the stories in the end. He'd tried getting away from the words, painting them out of himself instead—wasn't a picture worth a thousand words, after all—but they were stronger than he was. She, on the other hand, has entered into what she thinks of as an uneasy détente with the stories. She takes them into every part of her, literally into her very flesh, and in turn she is left alone. Or she always had been. Until now.

She remembers how timid Ruben had been. She'd worried about him, cooped up in his apartment all day. How did he get by? What did he live on? She'd never asked; he'd never told, and his death revealed no answers. No family came by, and the landlord, who hadn't know they were close, failed to mention he was hiring a cleaning crew to haul Ruben's effects to a dump. Coming home from class, she'd encountered them on a final haul and was able to save no more than a handful of his sketches.

She'd toyed briefly with the idea of moving into his apartment after he died, partly because she felt surprisingly bereft without him and partly because she felt sorry for the landlord who couldn't rent the place. But it was a college town, memories are short, and cheap accommodation's hard to come by. Soon enough a steady parade of kids rotated through the studio next door that she's never stopped thinking of as Ruben's.

Nobody stays there long, but that might be coincidence. College students move around a lot, after all.

His ghost isn't there; she knows that much for sure. She'd have been the first to know. After all, no one's stories were as compelling as those of the dead, and no needs so compelling as theirs to tell all before moving on. The dead Ruben seemed to have no stories; she supposes she would have none, either. Eating the tales of others leaves you with none of your own.

Haunted, the house is for certain, but every place is haunted, as is every person, and you need only to look into their eyes to see how much. Everyone grows more haunted with age but not every old person is more haunted than every young person.

She'd been lucky in her job, clerical work in the basement of a building on campus where she rarely comes into contact with other people and is left alone as long as she keeps her head down and gets things done. So they think she's a weirdo. The student workers in particular she imagines regarding her with horror. The brighter they burn the more she frightens them. *She is what I will turn into if I make the wrong choice. If I take the wrong classes. If I take the wrong job. If I take the wrong relationship. If I don't do the right things.* Most of them were too young to understand that all the right things in the world might not save them in the end.

At work, all day, she catalogues, she files, she makes photocopies and fills out forms and hits "send" on emails. Things tick along regularly and predictably and twenty-odd years ago she'd never have imagined that such regularity, such boredom, such routine, could move her to tears of relief. The safety and security of it all. The way it buffers her against the world outside.

The world outside, and the thing that is drawing nearer to her. Sometimes she dreams of its footfalls in the corridor outside her apartment. Sometimes it taps on the window to be let in. Alone in her fortress of words she recites poetry to keep it out. The intoxication of the language seizes her, and she finds herself speaking in tongues, the verse of the ancients, the verse of forgotten people and lost races, the stories that had been lost.

Something is coming to retrieve them, and she does not want to let them go.

Everyone had thought she and Ruben were lovers, but they were not. The thought had never crossed their minds, in fact; they were something better. They were best friends. Despite the little they'd known about the mundane details of one another's lives like where they came from and what they'd been like before and who their parents and families were, they couldn't have been closer. They went in drag to parties, dressed in one another's clothes, answering only to the other's name. One bright morning they'd woken in the cemetery across from campus with no memory at all of how they'd gotten there the night before. Shaking with laughter at having eluded the sexton, they stole flowers from the graves to wear in their hair and ran all the way down to the Blue-bird Café for a breakfast of omelettes and big dense biscuits with apple butter. Later, after he died and the gift passed to her, she'd wondered at first how he'd managed to sleep in a cemetery at all with the dead all about, but she'd quickly learned that of course there are no ghosts in cemeteries; why would they linger in a place that had no meaning to them?

She hadn't understood then why Ruben gobbled hallu-cinogens like they were aspirin, acid and mushrooms and ecstasy, building a tolerance so high he started joking he had to keep them in his system just to stay in touch with reality. It wasn't a joke. What had been such a carefree time for her had been a final, desperate, losing bid for survival on his part. In the end, she hadn't been enough to save him.

Another letter comes through the mail slot, exactly one week later. This time she is standing in the lobby when it is pushed through, having just arrived home from work. She freezes as the flap clinks; she did not see anyone behind her as she came up the walkway, and she immediately tugs the door open, but the walkway is empty, and so is the sidewalk beyond.

She carries the letter up to her studio and sets it on the little table in the kitchen while she boils pasta and dumps some jarred sauce into a pan to heat. Then she sits and looks at the letter for a long time.

The last time she had received letters like these, Ruben had just died. At first she hadn't understood what was happening to her. His curse had come to her first in dreams, dreams that belonged not to her but to other people. There is, she learned, no mistaking other people's dreams for your own. It's not the content but the substance that is wrong, the grammar of other people's subconscious. It was a horrific violation, and she woke sick and unable to get out of bed. She'd failed all her classes that semester and never made it back into school, but by then it didn't matter anyway; where would she have gone, what kind of life could she have built with this inside her?

The first message had arrived shortly after, dropped through the slot just like the last by someone who was clearly not the mail carrier, who came into the building properly with a key and left the mail for everyone stacked on a shelf in the foyer. The handwriting was shaky and old-fashioned. Five mundane words: *He gave you his gift.* She dropped it, shuddering. Out loud she said, "You might as well say 'he gave you smallpox'," but she didn't laugh after she said it like she'd hoped she might. She tried to be normal. She put on music and dressed up and went out to hear music like she and Ruben would have done together, but rather than trying her luck among the slim pretty girls and the earnest scruffy-haired boys she found herself slouched against the bar while a sad woman named Melanie rattled off a lifetime litany of abuse and bad luck to her. Melanie was pretty, dark-haired and dark-eyed, but this was not the kind of intimacy she was looking for; this was raw and shocking and real. Still, she misunderstood it, and took Melanie home with her, and woke in the night to find her crouched at the foot of her bed staring at her. "There's something inside you," Melanie said. "Something's wrong." She dressed and left and Aisha never saw her again.

She had begun to simultaneously attract and repel people like that; she knew it. They wanted her for the space of their stories and then no more. She somehow had not noticed she'd been Ruben's only friend, because they'd been so close there'd been space only for the two of them in the intense few months they spent together. That's how Ruben had known. How he had known he could let go and give it to her. She told herself it was not a betrayal. She told herself Ruben had not done it to hurt her. She told herself Ruben had done it because he'd known she was stronger than he could ever be.

But these days, she feels twice her age even if she looks half it. She feels the stories now are writing themselves upon her organs, that if she were sliced open, her heart and her liver and her bones would be covered in words.

11

In those early days, there had been two more letters in quick succession and then none until it all started up again. The second had been another single word framed by the expanse of creamy white all around it: "Atavistic". Well, that was helpful. She was a throwback. A shaman. She could hang herself a shingle and charge money and promise to channel people's spirit guides and go on television and weep while holding the hands of the mothers of lost children. The third was an actual letter, two pages covered in the shaky old-fashioned handwriting. She'd read it through once and burned it, willing herself to forget most of it. Over the years she had regretted her actions many times, but what was life made of if not hasty actions and years of regret? If she'd learned nothing else from all the stories she'd heard, she'd learned that.

The third letter had been an apology, of sorts. Or so she thought. Its language had been so elliptical. It had been like reading the writing of someone who not only lacks English as a first language, but lacks facility with any language at all. She had burned it because it did not shed any light on her circumstances, on the hows and the whys. And yet there might have been clues in the letter, clues that in those early days passed her by.

She cannot bring herself to open the most recent letter, not after more than two decades of silence from them, whoever they are. That night in her apartment, the pasta had boiled over and the sauce had burned to the bottom of the pan while she sat and stared at it. She went out and bought a pack of cigarettes and smoked half of them, still staring at it, telling herself with each one she would open it *now now now*. She went out a second time and bought a bottle of wine and drank it down but she'd known better; as with Ruben, such substances barely touched her. In fact, afterward she felt more alert and on edge than before.

She carries the letter to work with her the following day; afterward, she sits in the sun outside a restaurant on Broad Street, which is choked with traffic. She needs to be in the world in order to confront what is inside the envelope.

She raises her head and looks all about her. *The trouble is, the town has changed and I have not. Everything has changed except me.* All the old stories are right; eternal life is a curse, not a blessing. Only the words carved on her flesh mark the physical passage of time. However ancient she feels in her soul, when she looks in the mirror she sees only a slightly maddened version of the Aisha that she's always been. The past twenty-five years have been agony; how many more quarter-centuries can she bear to count off before she gives up? How many had Ruben endured? How had she, who believed herself his truest intimate, known so little of the truth about him?

For now, her family jokes about her hiding a picture in the attic to ensure eternal youthfulness, or sleeping in a bed of graveyard dirt, but how long will it be before she will have to cut ties entirely and move on, disappear? And how *does* one disappear any longer? It's not like in ages past: a name change, a new town, a new country even, and a whole new identity. The modern world ensures your identity clings to you as surely as your fingerprints.

And then there is the hunger; oh, God, the hunger for people's stories, and how it mingles with repulsion until she is unable to distinguish one from the other. The insatiable lust for the most troubled or repellent pieces of people's past leaves her shaken and ashamed and starving for more. She knows what she is: it might not be blood that she drinks, but the effects are the same save for the fact that she does not leave a trail of dead behind her. No, if anything, she is the victim, not them.

Enough.

In one swift move, she rips the letter open.

My Dear Aisha,

She recoils at the first three words. How dare they call her by name. How dare they refer to her as "dear" anything, as "my" anything. Whoever they are, she is not theirs.

A quarter of a century has passed since our brother, whom you knew as Ruben, chose to finish his association with our order and left us a sister in his place.

No. No. No. She is a sister to four siblings she loves; she is not sister to these monsters, whoever they might be.

We find that a quarter of a century tends to be something of a turning point, the stage at which our new acolytes begin to seek answers about the why and the what next of who they are.

A vampire identity crisis. But of course. The ultimate ailment for the modern age.

The first and most important thing that we want you to know is that you are far from alone. And that you have a choice.

Those words are the most surprising words she's encountered so far. She rereads them a few times to make sure that she understands them.

You have a choice.

She reads on.

Alone that evening in her apartment, she thinks about the letter, and the choice. Ruben had presumably been offered this same choice at some point; why then had he not taken it?

Giving back the words . . .

She can relinquish it all. She can let go of the words; abandon the eternal life; return to a normal existence. No more stories, no more solitude, no more hunger. A life, a family, everything she has wanted across these years, all of those things that had been denied her for so long.

In the shower, she huddles under the hot water spray and weeps, clutching her scars, willing them away, the words carved there. By tomorrow, they will be gone. The walls of her apartment will be pristine again. Her mind, her insides, her soul will be cleansed. It would be as though it never was.

For the first time in twenty-five years, her dreams that night are undisturbed.

Yet she wakes in a panic, not knowing why. The first thing she does, even before opening her eyes, is clutch at her flesh, pinching it and running her fingers over it, but it is too late. Her body is smooth and unblemished. The scars that have marked her for well over a decade are gone.

She is still dreaming. She must still be dreaming. She keeps her eyes clenched tight, willing the dream to end, but it does not. It will end on waking. She must open her eyes. It must be near midday, because the room is flooded with light, and her walls are cream-colored, her words gone.

"No," she says. "It isn't right. It isn't fair. It isn't what I wanted."

She says it hoping they can hear her—whoever they are—after all, had they not heard her desires, what she believed to be her desires, of the previous night?

But she was wrong. Whoever they were, why could they not have seen that, the desire behind her desire, the gap between what she believed she wanted and what she truly wants?

She dresses quickly, and clatters down the stairs. She was due at work hours ago, but work doesn't matter any longer. Outside, she staggers toward Prince Avenue. There has to be someone out here who needs to share a story. But passers-by ignore her, or seem to actively avoid her, and no wonder: she must seem crazy to them. It is all she can do not to clutch at them, shout at them to tell her their stories, to pour their pain into her and let its sweetness consume her.

Then she does grab a man by the shoulders—he has a story, a terrible one, she can tell from the eyes, she still has that much of her old self, at least—but he only stares at her, shakes her off with a "Crazy bitch!" and goes off muttering about her, glancing back once or twice to ensure she keeps her distance.

That's when she starts to weep, and to push up the sleeves on her shirt to stare again in horror at her unbroken flesh. Had this, then, been the moment that had destroyed Ruben? Not the burden, but its loss?

But *where* have her stories gone? Who has taken them on? Who has her power now? Why was she not allowed to choose a successor as Ruben had? Was it because she loved no one as she and Ruben had loved each other?

No one answers, because they aren't speaking to her any longer. She is no longer of any concern to them.

The woman at the rental car counter is tanned and perky. Aisha watches as she efficiently taps out codes on the computer keyboard. No insurance, thanks, back in a week (never), and she runs Aisha's debit card and hands over the keys and just like that Aisha is free, freer than she's ever been in her life. She points the car west and drives. Near dusk, she stops at a Denny's and eats a grilled cheese sandwich with fries, then gets back in the car and drives until she can't any longer. She isn't sure where she is when she pulls over to sleep for a while. In the morning she decides to get her bearings and purchase a paper map at the next service station.

Surely ghosts will still speak with her, even if the living will not. Surely she can find sites of savagery and mass suffering, Indian massacres and Civil War battlefields. Surely the dead will want her.

She had made a series of turns so far off the beaten path that she drives for some time without seeing any services or even a main road at all, and the gas gauge is dropping. Twice she stops at isolated houses and knocks on the door in hope of asking for directions, but no one answers; at one she hears a television inside, but perhaps she wouldn't answer a door to a stranger either, if she lived in the middle of nowhere.

(And yet she would, or she would have; letting in strangers was what she *did*. What she did now, who she was now, she could not say.)

At last a series of turns brings her onto a wider road, and then a three-lane highway. A gas station comes into view just as her gauge is slipping into the red zone. She fills up the car, and although there aren't any maps for sale, she gets directions back onto the interstate from the owner. She is, it seemed, somewhere in Arkansas.

Hunger, not for food, gnaws at her like the pain of a phantom limb.

Ruben's fate is not going to be her own. She doesn't need them, whoever they are. She can still get people to tell her their stories and she will learn how to hear ghosts on her own as well. She will figure out how to survive. Money, a place to live, those things are easy enough to come by. She just needs to get people's words. She just needs to disappear. For all she knows she might live forever after all.

Before she reaches the interstate again, she sees a small figure trudging along the side of the road, and she eases the car onto the shoulder. What she'd taken for a teenage boy is actually a girl of roughly the same age, a pale face ringed by jet-black hair peering out from a hoodie.

"I'll make you a deal," she says as the girl approaches her driver's window, mouth opening to query or beg. Aisha nods at the keys still in the ignition as she slides over into the passenger's side. "You drive. Anywhere you want to go. I'll sit here and you tell me about yourself. Tell me your story."

The girl hesitates. Aisha sees her looking for the catch; glancing around half in expectation of an assailant, furtively surveying the back seat, assessing the situation.

"No strings attached," says Aisha, "take it or leave it," inside, begging the girl to take it.

The girl presumably makes the split second decision that this was one gift horse she will not look in the mouth, shrugs a little at whatever fates she's consulted, and opens the driver's side door. "You can drive, can't you?" Aisha says, and the girl nods and, surprisingly safety conscious, goes through the motions of adjusting the seat, the seatbelt, the rear and side mirrors, before cautiously easing them back onto the road.

"Anywhere?" she says, and her voice is a backwoods drawl.

"Anywhere at all," Aisha says. "I've got all the time in the world. But remember your end of the deal. Before we get to where you want to go, you have to tell me your story."

Aisha lies back against the headrest and closes her eyes. The girl begins to talk, and above the comforting throb of the engine her accent and her story are as dark and as murky as the swampland she describes as her eastern Arkansas home. But there is some measure of hope in the story she tells as well; hope drove her out of the house one moonless night, after all; hope had her stick out her thumb in search of rides, hope made her get into Aisha's car and start driving toward a destination not yet named, but that didn't matter, because her story in all its pain and glory is spilling out of her and Aisha is right: she doesn't need *them*. The girl talks and talks and Aisha devours the words; she finds a ballpoint pen in the glove compartment of the car and begins writing them in tiny letters on the palm of her hand and when she runs out of room she moves to her forearm and when there is no more room there she moves to her knees, her calves, and the girl doesn't seem to care because they never do once their stories get going. In the midst of the terror and despair of which they speak, the stories are beautiful. The words make them beautiful. The fact that a living tongue spoke them makes them beautiful. Aisha cannot wait to live inside them again, to ruin her flesh with their substance again, and what will become of her now she does not know, but she also knows that it does not matter because the stories will always be, written on her bones, the very filaments that string her soul together and keep her anchored to this earth.

Widdershins

Tuesday

I'm told there is a path, and a gate, and beyond it a spring, but so far I haven't been able to find any of it. I tried to find it yesterday and ended up in the forest. I keep ending up in the forest.

I came to this corner of Ireland to get away from myself, or find myself, I'm not sure which, after I crashed and burned my career and my family and everything that mattered to me back home in Oregon. If you've lived in Portland you've heard of the ad agency where I used to work, and if you've lived anywhere you've seen our—their—commercials, and yes, it ended badly, just like everything in what had, up to that point, been something of a charmed life. I was asked to leave my job not long after my wife left me for an airline pilot and moved to Toronto with our two daughters. Well, the daughters weren't *really* mine—they were hers from her first marriage—so I didn't have any say in where they went. But they *were* mine, too, I loved them like my own. So a year ago I was a successful, still youngish guy with a prestigious career and a gorgeous family, and today I'm an aging dude mucking around a part of Ireland even Irish people have barely heard of. Ch-ch-ch-changes, as the song goes.

The light here, when there's light, is lovely. Mostly, it's dark and gloomy, which suits me.

Eoin was an old friend from college. That was a long time ago. He'd gone back home to Ireland after he finished

20

school in America, but we'd kept in touch off and on over the years. He and his partner Mary bought some property up here in the midlands where Mary's family originally came from. Right now they're up in the hills living out of their camper, breaking some preliminary ground on their unzoned and, I presume, illegal cob house. For the month of May, Eoin had offered me the run of the cottage they were renting. It's an old stone cottage—sounds romantic, but it's cold as death and the only heating comes from the coals I burn in the fireplace. Come in the spring, Eoin had said. The weather's best then. I don't know if that was some kind of Irish humour or what, but it's rained almost every day since I got here. The cold gets to me but the rain's not so bad, really, not that different from Portland. Luckily I like walking in the rain, so I go out every day looking for the gate. Eoin and Mary will be back down the mountain at the end of next week and if I haven't found it by then they can show me where it is.

The village isn't too far from me, a single street with a few shops down at one end and a row of more stone cottages at the top. Locally they're called the "railway cottages" because a railroad used to run behind them, though there's no trace of it now. It's said the inhabitants were so poor that the children would run out and steal coal off the train when it passed. Today the cottages are brightly painted and sport colourful window boxes. Two are rented out as holiday homes. People come here to fish and drive boats up and down the canal, probably more than ever since the Celtic Tiger died mid-leap. I think foreign holidays have fallen off the agenda for a lot of people these days.

In the village there are eight pubs, three butchers, a grocery, a produce place, a hardware store—everything you could need, really. Even a library, and Eoin's lent me his card.

I don't visit the village much, though. Mostly, I walk. It's good for thinking, and I used to make my living thinking, coming up with new ideas and new ways to get people to spend their money. So I keep imagining that I can think my way out of this hole I find myself in. And I look for the gate.

I don't know why I'm so obsessed with finding it. I heard about it the day after Eoin and Mary went up the mountain. I was in town to get a few groceries and I stopped in at one of the pubs and a farmer started chatting with me—people are friendly like that here, and not many tourists, foreign ones I mean, come through these parts, so they aren't sick of us. And the farmer said, oh, you're staying up near the old Kelly place and I said yes and then well, I don't know, because I didn't, and he said, aye, it's the old Kelly place.

If you go walking, he continued, there's a spring on the property, full of fish (if you can find it). He said, your man there can tell you all about it, and he pointed at the bartender who looked even older than the farmer and the bartender just looked at us and went back to whatever he was doing, talking to some guys at the other end of the bar, and the farmer laughed and I felt like it was a joke everyone was in on but me.

You walk south, the farmer told me, and you'll come to a path. And you follow the path and you'll come to an old stone wall with a wooden gate built into it and you open the gate and pass through and you'll come to the spring and if you like fishing you'll find plenty of it.

Do I like fishing? I don't know. I did as a child. I don't know anything right now, though. I'm no longer the man I was. I don't know who I am anymore.

I said, Yes, I like fishing, and he said, oh, that's too bad, then.

Wednesday Night

It's the middle of the night. I haven't looked at the time because I know it would depress me. I woke from a nightmare, clawing at the duvet, and I can't fall asleep again, and it's so cold in here, too cold to get up and try to get a fire going. How can it be May? It's like the dead of winter. I thought I heard something on the roof of the cottage. It's probably nothing, or maybe it's the rooks, those noisy birds that scared me the first few mornings I heard them shrieking outside.

It's time to confess something I haven't even been able to confess to myself, but the middle of the night is when these things rise up and take you. I don't miss them. My wife Tanya, the children, Stephanie, who's ten, and her little sister Kimmie, seven. "My girls," I used to call them collectively, because that's the sort of thing you do. I ought to feel their absence like a great stinking pit inside of me, like a hurt that will never heal, but the truth is I miss what they represented and the life we made. I don't actually miss *them*, have trouble recalling their faces as I write this, and that probably is a clue as to why Tanya left me for the pilot. I miss the man I was when I had them in my life. The man with the beautiful wife, the beautiful daughters. This realization concerns me. Were they just interchangeable parts of me? I don't think so. I am not unfeeling. I had believed I'd loved Tanya and Stephanie and Kimmie deeply, but what I felt when I lost the job and the house and the family was most of all shame, embarrassment, a concern about what people would think of *me*.

I'm huddled here in bed, getting a cramp trying to write under the covers by flashlight (because it's so cold) and I am trying to make myself miss them to no avail. Maybe I'm traumatised. Emotionally numb. I'd seen a counsellor a few times as it was all falling apart, when I still had a job that would pay for such things. He used words like that to describe it. *PTSD*, he said; not just for combat soldiers any longer! Apparently your wife leaving you for a pilot is traumatising too. And that trauma leaves you out of touch with your feelings.

Or maybe I never had any feelings to begin with.

Thursday
I walked into town today, thinking I'd take a break from the search for the gate. I'm not really obsessed. I just don't have anything better to do.

I bought some coffee and some milk and eggs at the grocery store and put them in my backpack, and I stopped in at the pub again. The farmer was there.

"I see you haven't found the gate yet," he said.

I waved the bartender over and bought us both pints. "How'd you know?" I said.

The farmer laughed. "You wouldn't be here if you had."

A spike of anger surprised me. I can be a decent sport, but I guess wasn't in the mood to play the dumb American tourist today. "Let me guess," I said. "It's a gate to fairyland, and once I find it, and cross to the other side, I'll never be seen or heard from again."

The farmer put a hand on my arm. "Drink up, lad. I've a story to tell ye." I don't think anyone's ever called me a *lad* before. So I took a swallow of stout and I listened.

Friday
I didn't feel like writing anymore yesterday. The farmer told such an unpleasant story that I didn't want to experience it again so soon; I went to bed early and couldn't sleep for hours, in my freezing bed looking out the open curtains at the cold overcast sky.

When I did sleep my dreams were wrong. I dreamed of figures that rose from the earth and rose from the trees and rose from stone and came down from the hills and gathered outside the cottage in a ring and sang at me in low and ancient and terrible voices.

It was the fault of the farmer, the nightmare. The old Kelly farm, he'd said. Up near you.

I said, I don't know.

Good for you, he said. Sure you want to know?

Know what?

He nodded deliberately. Back in the 1980s, he said, there was supposed to be a—a kind of dance party up there. They had a name for it.

A rave?

That was it, he said. And folks came from all over the place, and there were some lads that wandered up past the gate with some girls.

He said there were old famine cottages up that way, and from the way he described things, with lots of leering and innuendo, it sounded like they thought it was a good spot to smoke a little hash and fuck the girls. Place was deserted then, too. Owner fucked off to America decades ago. Or maybe England. Who knows? Gone, anyway.

Had they talked to anyone local, the farmer said, they'd have been warned away. They'd have been told not to go through the forest and past the gate. If only they'd bothered to ask.

The farmer leaned in close to me. "They found them," he said, "or what was left of them." Only then did I notice his bad breath, and the ring of rotted teeth remaining in his mouth. He made some sounds that I realised were laughter. "What was left was their heads, and some arms. They were in the forest. The parts that were left were hung from trees in the forest. What was done to the girls was even worse."

I said, "Oh, God."

"It got out," he said. "What was in got out for a little while but people drove it back behind the gate."

I noticed then that the others all sat together, and away from him. It occurred to me that maybe that was because they didn't like him. I don't like him much either. I took a sip of my stout and it was foul, as though his story had turned it rancid.

"It's true," the farmer said in the direction of the bartender, "isn't it?"

The bartender looked down our way and made a gesture with his head in which I could have read either agreement or dissent. I didn't wait around to learn any more. I shoved the drink away and stumbled out the door. I thought I heard laughter behind me, though I couldn't be sure, and all I wanted was to get away.

Monday

I spent the rest of Friday convincing myself they were fucking with me.

There was no path. There was no forest. There was no gate. Certainly, there were no entrails and soft bits of flesh strung from trees.

Friday night I did something new: I walked back into the village, looking for something to do. I ended up in a noisy kind of nightclub at the local hotel. Countless pints later I'd made a number of new friends, including Catriona and Gerry and Declan. The three proved to be adept at prying my life story out of me, or as much as you can while shouting over the beats of aggressive dance music. I said I'd blown my career and Gerry said it sounded like my wife was blowing something else and I laughed with them; did that mean, I wondered, that I was getting better? Or maybe just drunker.

They knew all about the gate, or claimed they did. Who the hell knows anymore? I can't tell when these people are pulling my leg and when they're being sincere. I'm not sure they can, either.

"Ah, the gate!" Catriona shouted. She was quite drunk at this point, blonde hair tumbling over in her red face as she leaned in toward me, vodka-and-something sloshing from the top of her glass. " 'Twas a witch that built it!"

"No, a druid I heard," Gerry said. "It's built in a what-do-you-call-it, a grove. Trees from a sacred druid grove. And when it starts to rot people go up there and rebuild it again."

"Who?" Catriona yelled. "What people?"

"I don't know!" Gerry shouted back, and they both dissolved into drunken laughter.

"I don't know any druids," Catriona shrieked, "do you?" and they were off again.

"It's a load of shite is what it is," Declan snapped. "It's a fuckin' gate built by a fuckin' farmer to keep his fuckin' sheep from running away. Wasn't never no fuckin' ravers murdered up there or witches or druids or curses or fuckin' leprechauns either." He stalked out after that with a cigarette in his hand. I found him sheltering from the pouring rain under the awning outside, smoking moodily.

I said, "Look, if I offended you back there . . . "

Declan spun on me. His eyes were wide. "Offended me. Offended me? If I offended you, he says!" He imitated my voice, my accent. "Stupid fucking blow-ins. Stupid fucking Americans. With your stupid fucking ideas about shamrocks and bombs and fucking charming little Irish people and what the fuck was that? *Druids?*"

I said, "But I never said anything about druids. That was the others," and by the look he gave me I knew I'd missed his point but I was too drunk to figure out how. He threw down his cigarette, pushed past me and was off up the road.

I went back in to join Catriona and Gerry and at first I thought they'd taken off, but finally spotted them making out in a corner. I left the nightclub with the dry stale taste of alcohol still on my tongue and the hangover already kicking in.

Going home in the dark was more difficult than I'd imagined it would be. No moon in the sky, and I kept stumbling over my own feet. Every once in a while a car would careen past me.

Naturally, this seemed like the best time imaginable to go looking for the gate.

And so rather than tucking myself into the freezing bed to shiver until dawn, I went looking for the path. I have never known a night so dark, and yet somehow I found the path immediately. Far in the distance I could hear something calling, maybe an owl, I don't know. It scared me so I started singing. I can't remember what I sang. I can't remember how I got to the gate.

Well, first I was in the forest, as always. The path before me narrowed as it always did and the trees closed in. And then I stumbled from the dark tunnel of trees and the moon passed from behind the clouds and spilled light all over the land and there it was, a wooden gate, closed, and on either side of it those stone walls you see all over Ireland. Beyond it, some crumbling stone cottages.

I put my hand on the gate. I felt the weight of its age.

I hesitated for just a moment before passing through. I hadn't really been joking when I said to the farmer that it was the gate to fairyland. I was afraid if I walked through it I'd be changed somehow. But wasn't I already changed? Hadn't I already walked through that metaphorical gate of life? Jesus—or *Jaysus*, as they say in these parts—I'd clearly had too much to drink, coming up with stupid shit like that.

I pushed on the gate. It resisted, and I realised I needed to lift it a little using both hands. And then it swung open before me. It was just an ordinary gate, and the other side was ordinary too.

I walked about a little bit. I poked around the derelict cottages. The floors were muck. You could get stuck in them. I couldn't imagine anyone thinking going up there to get laid was a good idea, not unless you had a fetish for freezing mud. If anything gave lie to the farmer's tale it was that. The whole place altogether depressed me. I wondered why I'd been so anxious to find my way there in the first place.

Still, I wanted to find the stream as well, to see if it was all truly as the farmer had described it, so I made a wide circle round the cottages and headed downhill. I could hear the water running before I found it. I can't say if it was stocked with fish as the farmer had claimed—the moonlight glistened on the surface but didn't penetrate—but what surprised me was the discovery that someone had been there recently, several someones by the look of things. A circle of stones like seats ringed the remains of a fire, and tent pegs lay scattered nearby.

I stepped closer, and saw that where the moonlight fell, one of the trees had been scarred by carvings, mostly names and crudely drawn stick figures but one unfamiliar word as well: *tuaithbel*.

As I traced the outline of the letters with a finger, I heard something rustling nearby. I turned and saw it watching me from some brush. It was something—well, it was a fox. It must have been a fox. Its mouth opened; I'd have sworn it was struggling to summon some awful parody of human speech at me. Its tongue was very long and very red.

I hadn't realised they have such sharp, cunning faces.

Tuesday
I don't know how I made it home that night, and I don't remember the rest of the weekend. But every morning I've woken with that word on my tongue: *tuaithbel*, along with a hollowed-out sense that pieces of my dreams were stolen from me while I slept.

Yesterday I walked back into town to use the library's internet service. It was drizzling and by the time I arrived I was wet and even colder than usual. I couldn't bring myself to ask the librarians about the murder—it seemed too vulgar, if a lie, and too raw and horrible if true. I tried a variety of search terms and found nothing at all. It's unlikely that such a bizarre event would have faded into obscurity.

Tuaithbel yielded more answers. I scanned the first page of results without clicking on any of them. "Against the sun," one snippet from an Irish dictionary explained, and from another, "left-hand, anti-clockwise, widdershins. To curse someone go *tuaithbel*." The rest of the results on the page were in Irish.

Widdershins. I had a vague memory of once doing a campaign for a small clothing company bearing the name; I knew the word without bothering to know what it meant and I'm sure they didn't really know either. They probably just thought it was a cool word. I googled that, too. *To go counter-clockwise. Bad luck. Opposite the sun's direction.* I'd have advised them to choose a different name, had I realised.

I sat back in my chair, rubbing my eyes and trying to remember in what direction I'd walked round the cottages. Had I gone *tuaithbel?* Did it matter?

With the librarian's help, I found a book that included some information on sacred trees. I read about the magical properties of oak and ash and hawthorn. I wondered what ancient people had discovered something terrible in that place and how they'd built the gate to keep it on the other side. Maybe ever since, people had kept rebuilding even though they no longer knew why, just as the fertility of hares accompanies Easter, and Christmas brings celebrations of light against a darkness no one believes in any longer.

Maybe it hadn't been the famine at all that drove people from the derelict cottages. Maybe it had been something else entirely.

I needed a drink.

I need one now. I know there is something at the window, looking in at me. It hides when I turn my head but it leaves its shape behind on the glass to frighten me. Its shape is a wrongness. All about the cottage is the smell of something that has been old and lost for far too long.

Tuesday. Later.

I went outside, but I could hardly see a thing. Something rustled in a hedge. It turned out to be a fox. Just an ordinary one this time.

I'm very frightened. I came back in, and I've found someone has been in the house. Someone took pieces of coal and wrote that word all over the walls. *Tuaithbel*. Who would have done such a thing? I wasn't even out that long. Well, I don't think so. Perhaps I was. Perhaps.

My own hands are so thick with coal dust. It's smearing this paper as I write. I can barely see the words now even as I set them down. It's because I was trying to rub out the words on the wall with my hands. I didn't put them there myself. I wouldn't do that.

After I left the library today, I went back to the pub. I took my usual spot at the bar. The farmer, for once, was nowhere to be seen. The bartender came over to me, his face as expressionless as ever.

"Where's . . . ?" I made a gesture toward the farmer's usual spot.

The bartender just looked at me. "I don't know who ye mean," he said.

I got angry. "The guy!" My voice was too loud and sounded very flat and very American to me. The men at the other end of the bar were staring. "The guy I talked to here!"

The bartender said, "You should leave."

"You know who I mean!"

The others were all older and smaller than me, respect-able-looking in neat but worn sweaters and honest soiled hands. They weren't getting up from their stools yet, but they were wary, and had the look of men who knew how to handle themselves if needed. I can take a hint. I left.

Tuesday. Later still.

I am remembering now something Mary said to me off-handedly when I first got here. I'd forgotten it, the way you do, because it didn't matter at the time. They'd got the place very cheap, she said. There'd been a farm here and then the farmer up and left decades ago, seemingly overnight. And the place had been abandoned ever since.

"It was weird," Eoin said, hearing our conversation as he was coming in from outside and stomping the mud off his wellies. "Sure, people emigrated all the time, but not old country farmers, and not suddenly, and not for a reason like that."

"What was the reason?" I asked.

Mary said, "My mam remembered when it happened. It was said because of something he found in the earth, while tilling his fields. Something that upset him so that he went away forever."

"Something? What kind of something?"

"He wouldn't say," Mary told me. "He said it wasn't made of metal and it wasn't made of stone and it wasn't anything he could recognise. At first he took it out of the earth and brought it into the cottage. He thought it might be some-thing historical, you know, something valuable. He said the night that he brought it into the cottage he passed the most terrible night of his life. That was all he would ever say about it, except that he buried it back again where he found it."

And then the roast was ready so we took it out and Eoin poured the wine and we all forgot about the farmer and his find.

I should have remembered that. I should not have sought the gate.

Wednesday

Dawn comes early here. It's Wednesday morning that still feels like an endless Tuesday because I never slept. Just past daybreak, and it's going to be a rare clear morning as evidenced by the soft blues and sunrise pastels smearing the sky. I'm writing this in the back garden, propping my notebook on the little stone wall that encircles it. The air is crisp and clean and everything feels new. The light is magical. It's the kind of day you'd wake to and know whatever you'd faced up to that point, and no matter what happened, everything was about to be okay.

It is the kind of morning that makes up for everything. It makes up for all the pain of being alive. It is the kind of morning so beautiful that it is enough.

And that matters, because it may be the last morning for me.

Rather than sleeping, I had dreamed with my eyes open and my senses about me. I had dreamed about something a young Earth made wrong, something that then hid itself *in* the Earth, and found itself trapped. I dreamed about something that could sleep for a very long time and wake hungry. Always hungry.

I dreamed about people who would design rituals and protocols to ensnare it, or imagine they had done so. Who can say that it mattered which way I walked round the cottages. Who can say whether the oak and the ash and the hawthorn made any difference. In the end, we all find ourselves in the same place.

Sooner or later we all go widdershins.

Whatever it is that I unleashed the night I found the gate, it's been driven back before, so it can happen again. I don't really know how it's done. I doubt anybody does anymore. But I'm so hollowed out I imagine that if there is any old knowledge left to fill anyone when the time comes that it can fill me, that I can act as a sort of vessel for whatever protection was left there long ago by wiser folk. It's no great loss to anyone if I don't return.

I am leaving this book behind just in case. I don't know in case of what. I don't know if it will do any good. I don't know that anyone would or could believe anything that I've written here. Soon it won't matter. Soon it will all have ended, or it will not have.

I have never been a courageous man and I am not now. But the last waking dream I had was of a different Earth, of an Earth that might have been, or maybe an Earth that was or is or will be. An Earth that belonged to them. A braver man would not risk the stringing of his own beloved skin and soft organs through the indifferent trees. A braver man would take his chances and flee.

But they have the measure of my soul already. I am sure of it. And so I will attempt to walk them back through the gate, walk them widdershins, walk them *tuaithbel*, walk them back into the never-was that ought to never be. If I am lucky, which I used to be and am not any longer, I might save myself in the process, remaking myself, becoming whole again.

If only I can find my way back.

Back through the gate, and out of the forest, and walking with the sun.

The House on Cobb Street

Concerning the affair of the house on Cobb Street, much ink has been spilled, most notably from the pens of Rupert Young in the busy offices of the *Athens Courier*; Maude Witcover at the alternative weekly *Chronictown*; and independent scholar, poet, and local roustabout Perry "Pear Tree" Parry, Jr. on his blog *Under the Pear Tree*. Indeed, the ink (or in the case of Parry, the electrons)—and those from whose pens (or keyboards) it spilled—are all that remain today of the incidents that came to be known locally (and colloquially) as the "Cobb Street Horror". The house itself was razed, its lot now surrounded by a high fence bearing a sign that announces the construction presumably in progress behind it as the future offices of Drs. Laura Gonzales and Didi Mueller, D.D.S. The principal witnesses in this case did not respond to repeated enquiries and, in one case, obtained a restraining order against this author. And the young woman in question is said by all to have disappeared, if indeed she ever existed in the first place.

> – *Ghosts and Ghouls of the New American South*
> Roger St. Lindsay (Random House, 2010)

I wanted to embed the YouTube video here, but it looks like it's been removed. It was uploaded by someone bearing the handle "cravencrane" who has no other activity on the site. Shot in low quality, perhaps with someone's cell phone, it showed a red-haired woman in a grey wool coat—presumably Felicia Barrow—not quite running, but walking away from the lens rapidly and talking over her shoulder as she went. "Of course Vivian existed," she said. "Of course she did. She was my friend. That hack would print anything to make his story sound more mysterious than it is. Roger St. Lindsay, that's not even his real name." And then she was out of the frame entirely and the clip ended.

The snippet purported to be part of a documentary-in-progress known as *The Disappearance of Vivian Crane*, but little else has been found about its origins, its current status, or the people behind it, and it is assumed that the project is currently dead. Felicia Barrow was located but had no comment about either the project or the fate of the Cranes.

– *Under the Pear Tree* (June 26, 2010)
Perry "Pear Tree" Parry

Vivian wakes.

It is a night like any other night and not like any night she has known at all.

The heart of the house is beating. She can hear it, vessels in the walls, the walls that exhale with that life's breath that is just as sweet to the house's groaning floorboards and arched doorways and soaring cupolas as her own breath is to her; she can hear it, heart beating and moaning and sighing and "settling". That was what her mother used to call it, in the other old house they lived in way back when, her a skinny wild girl; and maybe "settling" was the right word for what that old house did, that old house that was never alive, never had a pulse and a mind and—most of all—a desire, but "settling" was the least of what this old house did. Vivian knows that if she doesn't know anything else at all.

This old house is not settling for anything. This old house is maybe waiting, and possibly thinking, and could be sleeping even, but never settling.

This house is getting ready for something.

She can feel that like she can feel the other things. She has watched cats before, how they crouch to pounce, their muscles taut, *rippling under the skin* it's said, and she thinks it now about the house—even though it's a cliché (phrases become clichés because they're true, she tells her students)—this house is doing it, tense and expectant, counting time, ticking off years and months and weeks and days and hours and minutes and seconds and fragments of seconds and fragments of fragments and soon time itself degrades, disintegrates, and dies.

And then the alarm is screaming, and Vivian wakes for real.

Waking for real had become an important benchmark, and sometimes it took as many as several hours for her to be certain she had done so. She would be standing up in front of a class of freshmen who exuded boredom and eagerness in equal parts, talking about narrative point of view in "A Rose for Emily", and the knowledge would grip her: *I am here, this is real, I am awake.* And then she would drift, like one of the sunlight motes in the bright windows, and the class would wait—their professor was weird, a lot of professors were weird, *I'm still wasted from*

last night, can I borrow your ID, did you hear, did you, did you—and the dull cacophony of their voices, familiar and banal, would bring her back but past that point she could never bring *them* back, and often as not had to dismiss the class to save herself the humiliation of trying and failing to re-engage them.

That the house was haunted was a given. To recite the reasons she had known this to be the case from the moment she crossed the threshold was almost an exercise in tedium: there were the cold spots, the doors that slammed when no breeze had pushed them, the footsteps that paced in the rooms upstairs when she knew she was at home alone. But Chris had been so pleased, so happy to be moving back home. He'd found the house for sale and fallen in love with it, shabby as it was, battered by decades of student renters and badly in need of much repair and renovation but a diamond in the rough, he was sure, and how was she to tell him otherwise? It wasn't just that neither of them believed in such things; that was the least of it. But to suggest that the house was less than perfect in any way was to reject it, and, by extension, him.

Chris, as it turned out, had noticed those things as well.

Authorities have ruled the death of 38-year-old Christopher Crane a suicide, resulting from a single gunshot wound to the head.

Crane shot himself at approximately 2 a.m. on Thursday, July 22, in the backyard of the house on Cobb Street in West Athens that he shared with his wife, Vivian Crane.

According to Chief Deputy Coroner Wayne Evans, investigators discovered a note of "mostly incomprehensible gibberish" that is believed to be Crane's suicide note.

Crane was born and raised in Athens, and had recently returned to Georgia after seventeen years in the Seattle area . . .

– "Crane Death Ruled Suicide"
Athens Courier (July 29, 2008)
Rupert Young

When you watched those movies or read those books—*The
Amityville Horror* had been her particular childhood go-to
scare-fest—what you always asked yourself, of course, was
why don't they leave? Why would anyone stay in places
where terrifying apparitions leapt out at you, where walls
dripped blood, where no one slept any longer and the ratio-
nal world slowly receded and the unthinkable became real?

Countless storytellers worked themselves into contortions and employed ludicrous plot contrivances to keep
their protagonists captive, and yet the answer, Vivian
learned, was so much simpler: You stayed because you gave
up. You succumbed to a kind of learned helplessness that
convinced you that the veil between worlds had been pulled
back and you could not escape; wherever you went, you
would always be haunted.

You entered into an abusive relationship with a
haunted house.

And of course, there was also Chris to be considered. If
the house did, in fact, capture the spirits of the souls who
died there, shouldn't she stick around to keep him company, in case he wanted to contact her, in case he needed
her for something?

But Chris had remained strangely silent on the subject;
he either couldn't or wouldn't talk to her. She found herself
growing angry at his reticence, angrier even than she'd been

at him in life, when the house and its ghosts first began to come between them, as he was pronouncing her anxiety within its walls "neurotic" and "crazy", not yet knowing all the while those same ghosts had their ectoplasmic fingers deep inside him, in his brain and his heart, twisting them into something she no longer knew.

He was soundproofing one of the downstairs rooms so he could record music there, and then he wasn't; he stopped doing much of anything at all, she later realised, save for going to work, network administering something or other, but even there—well, nobody was going to tell a suicide's widow that her dead spouse would have been fired in short order, had he not offed himself before that eventuality could come to pass. But she wasn't a professor of literature for nothing; subtext was her specialty. In every interaction with his ex-colleagues and former supervisor she read it: he'd been neither well-liked nor competent, she surmised, and yet that wasn't the Chris she'd known and loved and married and moved into the house with. That wasn't her Chris, the Chris with the still-boyish flop of brown hair in his eyes and penchant for quoting from obscure spaghetti westerns. Not her Chris with his left hand calloused from the fret of his bass and his skill at navigating not just computers but workplaces and the people therein. And not just work: he had a warmth and generosity toward his fellow musicians that never failed to stagger her (a tireless ability to offer constructive feedback on the most appalling demos and YouTube uploads, because, he said, assholes were rampant enough in the music world without his increasing the net total assholery out there). Nobody disliked Chris, or at least not until the final months of his life.

That was the Chris the house made.

The first time for her, it was the little girls.

They were the worst of all; they had come to her when she slept in the guest room, coughing and feverish. She moved there so as not to disturb Chris with her tossings and turnings, her sweating and chills. That first time, she woke and heard them, an explosion of vicious whispers like a burst of static, and one word distinguishable above the rest—*her, her, her*—and she never knew that three letters, a single-breathed syllable, could be weighted with so much hatred. Next she became aware that she could not move, that her arms and legs and indeed her entire body seemed clamped in a vise; and finally, she knew that the vicious little girls floated somewhere above and just behind her head. She could see them in her mind's eye: four or five of them all with wide pale eyes, pert little nose, mouths half-open to display rows of sharp shiny teeth.

The morning after, she attributed it to fever (although she was really not *that* sick), or something else, googled phrases like "hypnagogic hallucination" and "sleep paralysis" and gazed on the Fuseli painting until she could no longer bear the image of the demon on the woman's breast and the mad-eyed horse thrusting its demented face through the curtains. She drank her coffee, cycled to campus (a bad idea; she had to pull over for three coughing fits in the two short miles she rode), and forgot about it.

She didn't forget about it; she'd had dreams stay with her before, mostly the unpleasant kind, and she hated those days, haunted by her own unconscious. She knew instinctively this was different. This was something from outside her. She could not have produced objective proof to show to someone that this was the case. She knew all about the games the mind could play to make oneself believe in its wild flights of fancy. And she knew in the depths of her soul (in which she did not believe, any more than she believed

41

in ghosts or haunting) that the kind of words she'd googled and the daylight world with its prosaic explanations and even the most unwholesome depths of her own brain had nothing to do with the things that had stolen into her room that night and despised her with such vehemence.

She had always thought of hate as a human emotion, a uniquely human frailty, a condition from which we might have to evolve in order to survive. Never before had she considered the possibility that hate was the most essential thing there was; that the universe was an engine driven by hate, animals savaging one another, atoms smashing together, planets and worlds dying in explosions of rock and fire. And to have so much of that directed at her—*at her*. She sat stunned in her office at Park Hall, her eyes fixed on the fake wood grain of her desk, someone knocking and knocking at her door and she knew it was a student because he'd scheduled an appointment with her and yet she could not answer it, she could not move, she could only sit paralysed by her new-found knowledge, and at last the knocking ceased and went away and she wished she could, too.

The existence of Christopher Crane has never been in question. The roots of the Crane family run deep in the soil of Clarke County, and though Crane himself was away for many years, he was fondly remembered as one of the founding members of the indie/alt-country group the Gaslight Hooligans, who went on to moderate mainstream success following his departure.

At least, this is how I remember Chris Crane, as do a number of people I know, but others insist on a different narrative: that Chris Crane never left town, that the

Gaslight Hooligans broke up more than a decade ago after playing a few house parties and one or two dates in local clubs to indifferent reception. Same as hundreds of other bands that spring up here each year and are soon forgotten.

Sources online and off are mixed in their reportage, but one thing is certain, that at least two and possibly more conflicting versions of the life of Chris Crane are out there. This introduces a disconcerting possibility: that we are all, now, existing in a dubiously real and unstable present, one in which Vivian Crane was and was not, and the house on Cobb Street at the heart of it all.

> – *Under the Pear Tree* (July 9, 2010)
> not available on blog, retrieved from cache
> Perry "Pear Tree" Parry

It is six months since she lost Chris. Her best friend Felicity has come from Seattle to visit her, has been staying in the house with her and urging her to get out. She doesn't need to do anything big, Felicity says, but she needs to do *something* besides go between home and campus. (This awful home, Felicity doesn't say, this terrible place that took Chris and is taking you. But Felicity knows.)

But she's hiding something from Felicity, and she's increasingly sure Chris was hiding the same thing from her in his last days. It's something that happened just before Felicity arrived, and afterward she tried to make Felicity postpone her visit (forever), but Felicity was having none of that. Felicity thinks Chris's suicide had opened the gulf between them; best friends from the age of five gone suddenly quiet and awkward in one another's presence. Felicity has no idea that the gulf is so much greater than that.

43

Vivian does not know whether to be overjoyed or hor-
rified that she now bears physical proof that she isn't mad.
A week before Felicity's visit, she is sleeping in the bed she
and Chris shared. She has woken paralysed once again, and
something is screaming in the walls. This is not so bad; at
least it's in the walls, and not in the room with her. She lies
there and thinks about "The Yellow Wallpaper", a story she
has taught to countless freshmen, and the poor insane nar-
rator following the twisty patterns and the women creeping
beneath them. Thinking of these creeping women serves,
oddly, to calm her as the screamer eventually winds down,
perhaps because she is able to make them into academic
abstractions and symbols while the suffering of the screaming woman in the walls is so very real.

But it is not long before she senses a presence beside her,
in the very bed next to her, and this is so terrible that she
starts to shake all over in spite of the paralysis. If it were
Chris, she would be sobbing with joy, but it is not Chris. It
is something else. She cannot tell if it is male or female, or
neither, or both. The something else takes her hand, weaves
its awful fingers through hers in that intimate fashion, and
she realises that before now she has never known what *cold*
truly means. From the palm of her hand the cold blooms
into her wrist, up her arm, and then throughout her body,
and she thinks *this is my death* and knows they will find her
some hours or days later and pronounce it "natural causes"
without knowing there is nothing in the world so unnatural
as the thing that has hold of her in the bed at that moment.

And then it's gone; she's heaving and sputtering and
gasping and racing for the bathroom where she steps into
a scalding hot shower, pajamas and all (for she is afraid to
be naked), and she is scrubbing herself, shivering still, and
her now ungripped hand is cold, so cold, and that's when
she first uncurls her fingers from her palm and sees it there,

44

a scorched circular shape, and then she looks closer and notices the head of the snake in the fleshy part at the base of her thumb and realises what she is seeing: an Ouroboros, the serpent devouring its own tail. And she knows in that moment that she has been claimed by something terrible.

The house on Cobb Street possessed several unique properties in regards to its purported haunting. There appeared to be no originating event, no horrific murders, no ghastly past prior to its possession of the Crane couple (and after reviewing the evidence, I believe this is indeed the best description of the effect the house had on Christopher and Vivian Crane). Locals remember no unsavory legends attached to the house. For roughly three decades prior to its purchase by the Cranes it was simply another decaying student residence. The house was previously owned by two sisters, who spent their entire lives there. Its Wisconsin-based owner, a great-niece who died shortly after the Cranes purchased it, left its management to the local Banks Realty, who say no unusual problems were ever encountered beyond the usual wear and tear.

Yet few of its residents from the years immediately prior to the Crane purchase could be tracked down. Of those who reported any paranormal experiences at all, each attributed it to the ingestion of psilocybin mushrooms or LSD. All three were located as inpatients at separate mental health facilities. None had been roommates with or were aware of the others, nor had any of them discussed their experiences with anyone else, but all date the onset of their initial mental illness as subsequent to their residence at the house on Cobb Street. Each claimed to have once borne a circular tattoo on the palm of their left hand, visible now only in the faintest outline of one of the three: that of the snake Ouroboros, the symbol for infinity.

It appears to have been a symbol with which Vivian Crane was obsessed as well, since, following her disappearance, numerous versions of it were said to have been found scratched on the walls throughout her house. This evidence, combined with the temporal shifts reported by Ms. Crane and all three of the former residents interviewed, originally led this author to theorise that this particular "haunting" is an occurrence on the order of "freak" weather events such as rains of frogs, sudden tornadoes, and so on. In other words, not ghosts at all, but an anomaly in the very fabric of time and space, burst into existence at some stage in the last few years. And the Ouroboros symbols suggest some sort of intelligence lurking behind this anomaly, something perhaps even more fearsome than the ghosts that populate the rest of this volume.

> – *Ghosts and Ghouls of the New American South*
> Roger St. Lindsay (Random House, 2010)

I've been reading Roger St. Lindsay's account of our local haunting, and reckless and inaccurate as his speculations appear to me (not to mention entirely ignorant of the laws of physics, and this apparent even to myself who knows as little about the topic as anyone), his method is not entirely one of madness. His history of the house is more or less corroborated, although his theories do border on the ludicrous. By the way, an alert reader recently forwarded to me the details, available only with a "pro-level" subscription, of an IMDB page regarding the documentary *The Disappearance of Vivian Crane*. Currently Vincent Llewellyn, who made his name with the *Poltergeist Rising* series of fictional "found footage" horror movies, is attached to the project. Apparently, however, production on the Crane documentary was halted due to legal concerns.

– *Under the Pear Tree* (August 12, 2010)
Perry "Pear Tree" Parry

Vivian wakes.

It is not a night like any other night. At first she cannot be certain why this is the case, and then she realises: it's because of the silence.

This is a terrible thing. Like the silence of children up to no good, except this silence is sinister, not mischievous. She reaches to touch Chris, and of course he is not beside her. She does this almost every night, but this time it reminds her of that other night. The last night. She had not been immediately concerned—why should she have been?—even though it wasn't like him to be up in the middle of the night, but then Chris had not seemed much like himself for some time. That night she reached for the lamp, and in the little pool of light she found her robe. She peeked into the guest room and at the sofa and Chris was nowhere. She went through the house looking for him, still not concerned, because none of it seemed real although she was certain it was not a dream.

Back up the stairs and down them again. It was here she began to call his name, here she started to get really worried. She wanted to be angry, because angry was better than worried, and she thought that she would be angry later, after finding him, angry at him for frightening her and happy for the chance to be angry because it would mean nothing was really wrong.

Later the questions would come, disbelieving: how could she have slept through the shotgun blast? Had she been drinking? Did she take drugs? Sleeping pills? Did she and Chris have a fight beforehand? They needn't have blamed her; she blamed herself. *How could you not have known, how could you not have done something, how could you, how could you?*

She had not been the one who found him propped against the back fence, his head ruined; a neighbour phoned the police shortly after it happened, reporting a gunshot, but this could not be possible, for she walked up and down the stairs and from room to room for hours, searching for him, long before she stumbled into a backyard awash in spinning lights and the sound of police radios and a cacophony of panic.

Some nights, the best nights, the police never arrived. On those nights she searched until she, Vivian Crane née Collins—born Vancouver, Washington June 10, 1971, raised in Seattle, the shy bookish only child of a single mother (father present only following occasional bursts of paternal guilt)—ceased to exist, or became a ghost, if that was indeed how one did become a ghost; she simply searched and searched the rooms, and the stairs, and the hallways again and again until she no longer remembered who she was or what she was looking for, and sometimes she woke and still could not remember for long moments where she belonged.

Driving Felicity to the airport in Atlanta at the end of her visit almost saved her. Almost. She remembered thinking that—remembered the hard and beautiful reality of Interstate 285 with its multiple lanes of frantic traffic, the billboards and the chain restaurants and the warehouses and the mundanity of it all. At Hartsfield, the busiest airport in the world, she stood in line at the check-in counter with Felicity and thought about sleek planes bearing her away to someplace, any other place, a place that was safe and far away, and then she saw Felicity through the security gate.

Afterward, she sat in the atrium in the main terminal for a while and chewed on a pesto chicken panino from the Atlanta Bread Company and thought about what to do next.

In the end it was all too overwhelming. *where would I go how would I explain to people what would happen to me, my job, my life, my belongings; I don't know any other way.*

And she got in her car and she drove back home again.

Chris's death had branded her as much as the Ouroboros symbol ever would.

So now she wakes to the silence of infinity. She has a singular thought, to leave the house, and it is so strong she wonders that she has not thought it before. She has been sleeping in a T-shirt and a pair of yoga pants (she used to take yoga, long ago when she also used to be a real person); to change, to even find her shoes would delay her disastrously, and her feet hit the floor with a thump and she is running down the stairs; she half expects the corridor to stretch out forever before her like a horror movie or a dream but the corridor is normal and the door springs open to her touch and outside the stars are reeling and she gasps lung-fulls of air that are not house-air and she is free; it is so easy, she need only not go back inside again. She doesn't have her keys (no time) so she cannot take the car, but she can run now, up the street, she can run forever if she has to, because even the simple act of breathing and running is an act of living and not one of extinction.

But here is nothing but silence. A dead, dark street, familiar houses blank and empty, no sound of traffic from the busy street a block away. No dogs barking, no sirens, nothing.

She will run back into the house and reset it; this time it will work.

Back inside the house. Deep breaths on the house side of the front door, and how has she not noticed the corrupted air, the choking rot and decay? Again she opens the door;

again she steps outside; again and again and again and again and she never imagined eternity like this, isolated even from her fellow ghosts, an infinity of repeating the same futile action again and again until time itself does die.

It is Athens's very own urban legend, one of short duration and dubious provenance, a tale of a woman who disappeared not only from her own life but from the lives of all of us. There is no record of her employment as an adjunct instructor at the university, though a few former students claim to recall taking her class. Chris Crane lived and died alone in the house on Cobb Street, although many insist this was not the case; some say his wife stayed there after his death, the wife in whom no one can quite believe or disbelieve in any longer. Some say it was she who was haunted, not the house, and she brought the haunting to all of us. Some say memory is forever shifting, never reliable; we take it on faith that we have lived all the days of our lives up to this moment.

But the handful of students who claim to remember Vivian Crane all produce the same account of the last day she turned up to class.

"She was going on and on about a snake eating itself, about time turning itself inside out and what would happen if you got caught in something like that, and where would something like that come from—God or another human being or just a natural force in the universe? And then she showed us this weird tattoo of the snake on the palm of her hand," says one young woman, who asked only to be identified by her first name, Kiersten. "And she said, 'What would it be like if reality had to constantly re-adjust itself in order to make things fit—what would it be like for the ones left behind?' "

This story is roughly the same as that told by two other individuals, both of whom asked not to be named or quoted at all. A fourth former student, who recounted a similar tale (with a few variations), has since recanted and asked not to be contacted again. When I attempted to follow up with the others I was unable to find anything about them. I did contact the student who recanted, despite his request, but he would not speak with me and indeed purported not to know me.

And so it goes: the mystery appears to be solving itself by scrubbing out its own traces until there will be no mystery left at all.

But Chris Crane was a friend of mine; we grew up together, we went to college together, we did stupid things together, and had he gone away for seventeen years and come back with a wife, surely I would be one of the first to know about it?

– "The Crane Enigma"
Chronictown (July 24-30, 2009)
Maude Witcover

She cycled home from campus that day as fast as she could, like she was outrunning something, even though she knew whatever it was could never be outpaced. She thought briefly of taking refuge in a church on the way; she had not believed in so very long that she was surprised at the tiny seed of comfort that began to unfurl deep in her chest when she thought it, but the only church she passed was the Southern Baptist one with the "all-trespassers-will-be-towed" sign in their parking lot and a dubious reputation with the progressive neighbourhood in which it sat, and she imagined its doors would be locked literally, no need for the figurative.

She rode as fast as she could but it is not possible to ride fast enough when infinity itself is at your heels.

A small assortment of reporters and curiosity-seekers were on hand today for the planned demolition of the house at the centre of what has come to be known as the Cobb Street Horror. The house had in recent months, following the disappearance of Vivian Crane, become a major nuisance for law enforcement and neighbours, as several self-styled "urban explorers" broke in to photograph the bizarre signs and symbols—purportedly left on the walls by Ms. Crane—and a series of mounting disturbances were reported in the vicinity. Said disturbances included the sound of a woman screaming, day and night; the sight of several little girls running from the front of the house; and a figure whom no witness could adequately or consistently describe in terms of sex, age, or appearance crawling about the perimeter of the house.

Although the "urban explorers" spoke of signs and glyphs and drawings of the now-famous Ouroboros throughout the house, none of them ever produced any identifiable photograph from inside. A number of photography methods were experimented with, from top-of-the-line digital technology to old 35mm film and even a Polaroid at one stage, but neither the least nor the most sophisticated technologies produced any images. Save for one. One resourceful young woman went so far as to construct a "pinhole" camera out of a cardboard box, and with that captured a single image: in a low right-hand corner near the front door, written in very small letters with a ballpoint pen (as the woman described it), were the words "This house erases people."

Paranormal investigators assert that the existence of this photograph supports the idea that Vivian Crane herself was trying urgently to convey something important to those who read it; if so, however, it was that one time only, for while others who entered the house reported seeing the graffiti, no one else was able to reproduce the pinhole camera's photograph, not even the photographer herself.

The demolition of the house on Cobb Street commenced without incident; in fact, it was so routine that bystanders quickly lost interest and dispersed.

— *Under the Pear Tree* (October 19, 2010)
Perry "Pear Tree" Parry

The heart of the house is lost. The heart of the house is beating. The heart of the house is bleeding. The heart of the house is breaking. The heart of the house is longing, mourning, searching, willing itself back into being, circles within circles, time turned inside out. The heart of the house, like all of us, is mad and lonely and betrayed.

From the e-book edition of *Ghosts and Ghouls of the New American South*, by Roger St. Lindsay, published with added material in 2012:

No unusual activity has been detected along Cobb Street since the house was razed and the dental offices built. The dentists at the site report a thriving practice. Today, fewer and fewer locals appear willing or able to talk about the incident in the house on Cobb Street.

The symbol of snakes twining round a rod known as the caduceus is sometimes used on medical signs although in fact this represents a confusion with the single-serpented Rod of Asclepius, and thus this author feels it would be ir-responsible to speculate about or attach any significance to the inclusion of the similar (if symbolically quite different) Ouroboros on the modest sign on the front lawn of the brick building. It ought, however, to be noted that on the day this author visited, several little girls were engaged in making similar chalk drawings on the sidewalk in front of the offices. On attempting to question them, this author was informed that they were not allowed to speak with strangers.

This author's sensitivity to the unsettling effects of their shrill voices and the flash of their fingers gripping the chalk and the sound of the chalk scratching at the sidewalk are all most likely attributable to the severe fever this author subse-quently suffered through in his hotel room later that night.

For now, we can only say that the house on Cobb Street has gone, and has taken its mysteries with it.

Where the Summer Dwells

L ittle was left now of the abandoned railway save for the rails themselves, two steel bars emerging from brambles and weedy clumps of grass. Seth, walking backward, followed them, clutching his camera, calling for Larkin to lie down between them so he could film her. The first hint of unease brushed Charlotte then, stroked her hair, caressed her cheek, and was gone almost as quickly—for no unease could exist here on this cloudless day, with skinny overeager Seth springing about, his hair flopping in his eyes, Lee perched on the hood of the car, head thrown back so his face was turned up toward the sun, and Larkin in her white eyelet sundress, stretched between the rails, arms above her head, miming bound wrists and revealing dark unshaven underarms, unexpectedly erotic.

Seth said, "Charlotte, give her your necklace thing to wear."

She knew what he was after: against Larkin's pale skin, the three copper disks would glint golden in the sun, but Charlotte, already wandering, pretended not to hear. The heavy grass, grown high enough to graze her fingertips dangling at her sides, scratched her bare legs. Seth said again, "Charlotte, Charlotte," but she didn't stop, snatching her hands back from the tops of the grasses and slipping her fingers round the disks.

She disliked seeing Larkin there where before it had been her and Cade and Victoria, lost in that summer a dozen

55

years ago now, happy times, when they'd finally been old enough to drive and they'd get lost on these back roads, looking for fallen-down houses and forgotten cemeteries, pulling off on abandoned sawmill lanes, listening to music like Elliot Smith and Andrew Bird—which had gotten them labelled fags at school. (*And how can you and I be fags? We're* girls, Vic had said, like the insult was supposed to make some logical sense.) In a collapsing one-room schoolhouse their fingers skated above the rotting keys of an abandoned piano. Cade found a pile of handheld fans in one corner, the kind funeral homes gave out with their addresses printed on one side and a crowd of pink-cheeked cherubs on the other. How did such things get left behind and forgotten, they asked one another. In what must have been the cloakroom, someone had started a fire at one point, for the wall was scorched beneath the rows of little wooden pegs. The forest had crept right up to the window; Charlotte had tried to imagine what scene the schoolchildren had looked out on one hundred years ago, but the past seemed remote, inaccessible, even in a place that was trapped there.

So long ago, and all of them grown up and gone away. She'd long known better than to come back here.

It had started like this: the day was born sticky and hot, and she and Lee and Seth and Larkin had stumbled into it—and into Seth's battered '79 Impala—early, just past dawn, out of the motel rooms they'd taken in exhaustion after driving straight through several nights. The shabby motel was just east of Muscle Shoals and bade them by way of copy board to SUPPORT OUR TROOPS and added that YOU'LL NEVER BE LONELY IF YOU "FRIEND" JESUS. Larkin, at the wheel, snorted, "Fanatics," but Seth said he got some good shots of it as they nosed out of the parking lot and back onto the highway. As noontime came and went and

56

they crossed the state line from Alabama into Georgia, the day had not improved. Charlotte thought stifling summer days in the South often felt old and stale, as though someone had forgotten to freshen things up, to air the place out. You'd be outside and wish you could ask someone to open a window.

Once they hit Bydell County, opening the windows had left them choking on clouds of red clay dust. Back in Oregon Seth had probably bought the Chevy for its white-trash hipster-chic aesthetic, and its lack of air-conditioning seemed negligible; here, as Lee pointed out, they faced a choice of asphyxiation by dust or dying of the heat like bugs trapped under glass. They had bounced along back roads, alternately coughing and sweltering, while the speakers crackled with the raw pickings of Mississippi bluesmen. Those guys—R.L. Burnside and T-Model Ford and Junior Kimbrough and all the rest on the Fat Possum label—those were the real sounds of the South, Seth said, at least before Fat Possum sold out and started signing all those indie bands instead. Never mind that the Delta was hundreds of miles to the west of them; the whole region might as well have been a figment of Seth's imagination, for all the resemblances his notions of the place bore to reality.

Charlotte had dutifully taken them to the places she recalled: the schoolhouse—now unsafe for entry, its roof caved in—and the Civil War-era cemetery with its toppling monuments and graves of former slaves granted the dubious honour of burial with the master, and the abandoned barn surrounded by junked farm equipment: rusted tractors and broken tillers. Seth shot it all with a bland enthusiasm, and then they'd crossed these tracks, and it was her own fault they were here. "Wait," she'd said. "Stop," she'd said. And so they did.

Back *then*, August had that winding-down feeling about it. The air remained sultry as ever; insects whirred in the brush and the sun rose relentlessly, day after day, as though it might never rain again. But they felt the end, Vic and Cade and Charlotte, felt the dark dull hallways of school-again looming near, the clanging lockers and the shrieking bells, textbooks on trigonometry, composition folders, laps around the gym, and smelly lunchrooms. The indignity of it all. *But not yet.* Some days still separated freedom from captivity. "We will make the most of it," Vic had announced, throwing herself back into the clover that grew wild and ragged along the train tracks. Cade was rolling another joint, flapping one hand at a persistent hovering bee, but Charlotte had a headache and didn't want to smoke anymore. "We should do something," Vic went on, "some kind of ceremony to mark this summer. To mark us all."

She made up the words. She was good at making things up. Charlotte could no longer remember what exactly Vic had said, but could still see her as she'd looked that day: red hair twisted on top of her head, wearing shorts and a black Neutral Milk Hotel T-shirt, and somehow regal despite it all.

Now Charlotte kicked at decaying ties, at scattered spikes. She had not been home in such a long time, and something almost like regret broke over her. Lee touched her on the back and made her jump.

"All right?"

She shrugged. He nodded. He always knew. They were closer than siblings. They plucked one another's thoughts out of thin air. He knew her better than anyone, better than any lover—and lovers always left her, claiming she held some part of herself remote from anyone's reach. She and Lee had met freshman year of their first day of college, when the housing department mistakenly assigned them to share a room in the co-ed dorm. Housing had reacted with considerably more horror than either of them and quickly found them gender-appropriate roommates, but they grew closer than siblings. Now Lee, exaggerating the Southern accent he'd left behind when they moved to the West Coast together, cried, "Oh mah gahd! It's a train track!" and they were both cracking up without really knowing why, because it was one of *those* jokes, its origins lost in time, probably rooted in mockery of someone they'd disliked but impenetrable to outsiders and now to them as well. While they were still laughing he said, "I'm sorry. You didn't have to come."

"No, don't be." She could imagine how events had unfolded before she entered the picture: the three of them, Lee and Seth and Larkin, getting high in Lee's living room and talking about Seth's idea for a documentary—something about the South (Seth had never been there) and a road trip, something he could enter into a film festival, maybe South by Southwest, when Lee, stoned and rash and half-in-love with Seth, blurted out Charlotte's name, said she'd be into it, she was between jobs now anyway and kinda depressed (he'd said something like that, she was sure of it). Lee had grown up in a faceless Atlanta suburb but Charlotte hailed from a hick town. *She* could take them into Southern Gothic country, all right.

The Southern Gothic that Seth imagined didn't really exist any longer, if it ever had, but he'd never know that. Nonetheless the three of them came pounding on the door of her Sellwood studio that same night. Five days and a world ago: it had been one of those idyllic Portland summer evenings, just warm enough for an outside table at the brewpub round the corner (to which the four of them had repaired, because Charlotte's studio was hot and stuffy and both alcohol and space were in short supply there). Safe in the lush green of a Pacific Northwest August, downing her third Ruby Red Ale, she could not remember the burnt-up humidity of Georgia in summer. Furthermore, she and Lee had both made the tactical error of assuming that Larkin, the only one of them with a real job—she worked at the advertising agency that made all the Nike commercials—would not be joining them. Larkin was okay but she had a way of assuming a blameless, bright, and superficial *let's-be-kind-to-the-help* sort of air whenever she talked. "It's *so* good to run into you," she would say, smiling brightly while somehow still managing to signal that the exact opposite was true.

At some point in the evening, maps had been produced, highlighters sketched ambitious routes along interstate highways. "It's freaky down there," Larkin warned, "*Deliverance* country," but nobody paid her any attention. By nine the next morning, when the phone jangled Charlotte awake, she was hungover and regretting the promises she'd made, but they were on their way over and backing out felt impossible.

Now Seth called back to them. "Let's follow the tracks! This is good stuff!"

"Excellent," Lee said. "Now he'll be hoping to encounter some backwoods eccentric he can get on camera."

"Some latter-day Hazel Motes."

"Nah, that's a little *too* eccentric. Maybe another Howard Finster. Religious fanatics are a lot more palatable when they're folk artists."

"And we grow 'em on trees here, those loveable eccentrics."

They watched the two for a moment. The sight of Larkin picking her way along the tracks in inappropriately flimsy red flip-flops made Charlotte feel meanly glad for just a moment. She said, "You know, it's a lost cause, darlin'. I don't care who else he might be sleeping with, he's utterly devoted to her."

"I know. I'm an idiot."

Charlotte shrugged again. "The things we do for love, right?"

That made him laugh. "You've never been in love in your life, how would you know? You're the one who does the heart breaking!"

"Shut up," she said, lightly, steadily. She'd never told him about Cade and Vic, which meant she'd never told anyone. "Let's go." Seth and Larkin went over a rise and vanished on the other side. They followed. A field stretched to the left of them, its grasses yellowing and dying in the summer drought; to the right, the ground dipped and fell away into already dead forest blanketed by kudzu.

When the kudzu covers something it leaves the shape behind and takes the thing itself down into the underworld, said Vic's voice in her head. Cade said, *My spooky girl*. Vic drew macabre sketches of things rising from the forest floor, of rooms empty but for unsettling shadows in wrong places, of faces that floated at windows and figures made out of bits of tin can and leaves and bones. She posted her work to her webpage, where it had lingered ghostlike for years until the free webhosting company shut down altogether. Charlotte used to visit there often, imagining that *this time* she'd find a message embedded somewhere in the pixels.

They'd thought to sleep out here under the stars that night. After half-an-hour of slapping mosquitoes they'd tried to squeeze into Cade's pup tent, without success. Since nobody could sleep, Cade pointed out constellations and told them fantastic stories about gas giants and collapsing black holes. When they ran out of stars to name, Vic took over the storytelling.

61

"Once upon a time," she said, "I came walking here when I was a little girl. I found these same tracks and I started to follow them. They took me deeper and deeper into a forest. I was growing tired and then I looked down and I saw that the metal rails had turned to bone. The bone was smooth and polished like someone took loving care of it. I wondered who would do a thing like that."

Cade said, "You didn't have to wonder long, though." He brushed damp strands of hair from her forehead.

"Not fair," Vic said, "you've heard part of the story before." Charlotte hated it when one of them reminded her it had been two of them before it became three of them, even though they meant nothing by it. Vic went on. "Three scruffy black dogs, uncollared, wild and hungry-looking, came slinking through the trees and waited a few yards away from me. Their flanks were thin and their ribs stuck out like this." Vic held her hands in a way that mimicked protruding ribs. "And then the biggest dog spoke to me. It wasn't a talking animal like in a children's story. It was the most awful thing I've ever heard in my life. It had blackened teeth and a blackened tongue and its voice sounded like something savage and wild and malformed."

Charlotte couldn't wait. "What did it say?"

"It said, 'Little girl, my brothers and I are going to eat you up. We're going to eat your feet first so you can't run away, and then we're going to eat your hands so you can't hurt us. We'll eat your stomach and your eyes, your elbows and your knees. We'll eat up every bit of you, slowly, and then we'll be filled up with pieces of you and you'll be part of us, Vic.'

"But what he and his brothers didn't notice was that while he was doing all that talking, I was filing my teeth into sharp needles. I filed my fingernails into claws and I took off my shoes and did the same for my toenails—he was

62

a really long-winded dog—and when everything I could make sharp was as sharp as could be, I made my move. I leapt on the talking one first and tore out its throat. Then I killed the others with my sharp new claws.

"By then I was all covered in blood and other awful things, and I wanted to bathe. I kept walking and I came to the railway trestle, and the river running beneath it. I took off all my clothes and I dived in, but while I was swimming I felt someone watching me from the shore. At first I thought it was just a water-spirit but then I knew for sure it was something else. So I came to the surface of the water and I saw a woman standing there. She was the most beautiful woman I've ever seen, or ever will see. I knew then that she was the one who cared for the tracks, who kept the bones polished and free of kudzu. She said, 'You have killed my three best companions.'

"I told her it wasn't my fault. It was kill or be killed, after all. She nodded and said that she understood but she had to take something from me anyway. She said that, and then she turned and started to walk away. I called after her, I asked her what she was taking. She said I'd find out one day."

"And did you?" Charlotte again, leaning forward, eager.

Vic said, "I'm still waiting."

Before they fell asleep at last Vic had suggested that they lay pennies on the tracks for trains to flatten, and even though they knew that nobody had used those tracks in decades, maybe a century, they did it anyway. They all heard the whistle in their dreams, and they woke to the sight of three smooth, flat disks balanced along the rails. Vic had scooped them up, laughing, and scraped little designs on them then and there, using her grandmother's diamond engagement ring that she always wore on her right ring-finger. In later years Charlotte wondered if Vic had done it herself, replaced the pennies with already-flattened ones

she'd brought with her. But they agreed they had all heard
the train passing, had felt the night air shiver, and anyway,
it wasn't the kind of thing Vic would do. She liked stories,
not hoaxes.

Seth and Larkin must have gotten farther ahead of them
than either Lee or Charlotte had realised. They passed over
the rise and saw no sign of them. Charlotte jumped when a
flock of birds burst from a nearby copse of trees and climbed
into the sky, shrieking. The only cloud they'd seen all day
passed before the sun; it lessened the heat's intensity but
left her feeling breathless and hemmed in. They walked
on. Ahead of them the railway vanished into a pine forest.

Lee put a hand up to his mouth and called, "Seth! Larkin!"

They waited. Only insects sang in reply.

In the forest, the needles felt soft and slick underfoot.
They had to leave the tracks in places where the undergrowth grew too thickly. Aluminium drink cans bleached
shiny and anonymous by the sun and rain littered the
railbed and gave way to other bits of garbage, twisted metal,
rotting lumber. They really should turn back now. Charlotte
felt it uncurling in her gut, the sense of crossing borders
into stranger places.

"I was in love," Charlotte said to Lee. "Once."

"You lie. What happened?"

"People leave," she said. "You know." It was almost true.

They had parted that morning in high spirits, filled with
plans for the week ahead. But Cade's parents had lain in
wait for him, as parents do. They sent him away—some
kind of military boarding school, maybe, or worse, one of
those boot camps like you saw on TV for troubled kids.
Vic's voice took on a bleak quality Charlotte had never
heard in it as she reported what little she knew. And then

Vic was gone as abruptly: IMs and emails went unanswered, the phone rang and rang for days, until at last Vic's mother answered it. She was doing fine, she told Charlotte in a tight voice, and she could talk to her friends when she was better. Vic messaged her once after that, hastily: "i did something stupid. tried to cut open my wrists." While Charlotte was typing a reply Vic added, "gotta run, they're back, they never leave me alone." Of course, Vic's mother had been lying; Vic had never returned to school that year, and Charlotte, so clearly *not our kind of people* in a way that made Vic's mother wrinkle her country-club nose, had not been told what became of her. And that had been the end of that.

Or so it seemed. The following summer, two weeks into a waitressing job down at Hilton Head, she'd gotten a phone call.

"It's an emergency," groused her manager Mac. He towered over her, all six-foot-five of him, in the narrow passage between the kitchen and the dining room where the staff phone was located. "Or it damn well better be."

"Char, it's Vic."

"*Is* it an emergency?" Mac demanded, hands on hips. "You know you can't take personal phone calls here!"

"Jesus," Vic said. "Char, listen, you have to come here tonight. Me and Cade are in town."

"Five minutes!" Mac mouthed, holding up a splayed hand, wiggling his five fingers in case she hadn't gotten the message.

"We're going out to the train tracks. I know how to get through. I figured it out."

Something metal clattered to the floor in the kitchen. Wes, the sous chef, shouted, "Fuck!" The kitchen door jostled her in the back. "Your table sixteen is up, Char!"

"Figured what out?"

"How to cross borders. How to get to the other side. On purpose this time, not by accident." Vic was impatient. "Meet us at moonrise. Sometime after midnight. We'll wait for you."

An abrupt click was followed by silence. Mac leaned against the wall, one finger on the phone's cradle. "Table sixteen wants their shrimp," he smirked.

Charlotte untied her apron and flung it at him. "Better take it to them." In the parking lot her heart raced. She called both Vic's and Cade's home numbers from her cell phone, but the lines on the other end merely rang and rang, as she expected. Bydell was five hours away and she had no idea when the moon would rise. At first luck was with her as she raced through the night, her headlights swallowing the centre-line and not a cop in sight. Outside of Augusta, disaster: the clean-up from a multi-car accident blocked every lane and she sat at the back of a long line of cars. Crawling forward, she could see highway patrolmen carefully waving motorists to detour one by one onto the interstate's shoulder, but by the time her turn came and she was moving at a steady speed again, the moon showed its face. "Waning gibbous," she whispered, knowing the words because Cade had taught her the moon phases like incantatory phrases. *Waxing gibbous. Full. Waning gibbous. Half-moon. Waning crescent. Dark.* She kept driving. She didn't know what else to do. Once she reached her destination, she sat by the tracks until sun-up. The first rays of light picked out something glinting on the tracks: their pendants. They had left her a message, but she didn't know what to do with it.

"The trestle's just ahead," she told Lee, but they spotted it before she finished speaking, its wooden planks spanning the gully below. Only a trickle of water suggested that it had once been a Broad River tributary. "God, this drought. It's like the whole state is gonna catch on fire." They walked to the edge of the trestle. Slats in the middle had rotted into the parched channel.

They both spun round at the sound of crashing undergrowth, and Seth's voice reached them. "Hey, guys! We got some great stuff!" He and Larkin made their way back over to the tracks. "That trestle," Seth said. "It's amazing. Like, almost haunting. Look."

He showed them a long shot of the trestle, standing some way upstream—or what would have been upstream, had there been any water. Next, a shot of broken boards, looking down into the ravine below. "I walked out to the middle," he said, "as far as I could go."

Larkin faked a shiver. "You made it look creepy."

Seth shrugged. "Hey, I think we're done here. I'm hungry. Are you hungry?" He turned to Charlotte. "You must know, like, some pretty cool place around here we could eat, right? Barbecue or something? Or like soul food?" He didn't wait for an answer but turned with Larkin and started back along the tracks.

"Right," Charlotte said, watching them go. "They're done, so we are too, I guess."

"I guess," Lee said.

She walked to the edge of the bank and closed her eyes. She could hear the soft whistle of the train approaching. She took hold of the pennies. In her hand they felt warm, almost alive. Maybe the train would slow, maybe Cade and Vic would lift her up into their arms. She could smell that summer coming nearer. It would be as though no time had passed. Why had she waited so long?

Lee touched her on her back. She knew it was Lee; she could smell his cologne.

"What really happened?" he said. "You were in love and then what happened?"

Charlotte opened her eyes. She said, "I think they went away with the fairies, you know? I just couldn't go with them."

The drone of the cicadas and the tree frogs rose to a crescendo, and fell again. She and Lee stood there, the sun dappling through the trees and onto their skin. Their arms glowed golden in its light. Behind them, the trestle groaned and creaked in a wind that did not reach them, and grew silent like the missing and the lost.

Who Is This Who Is Coming?

There was no train service to Happisburgh, so Fern Blackwell faced a choice of going the entire way by bus or taking a taxi from a nearby station. In the course of investigating which might be the more tolerable option she also learned that, as seemed to be the case with many English place names, the spelling of the village bore little resemblance to its actual pronunciation: *Haze-bro*, the woman at the pub where she booked a room gently corrected her over the phone. Fern wrote it down in her notebook so that she would not make the error again. She did not want, on her first and perhaps only trip abroad, to seem an ugly, ignorant American.

Once she had settled on train and taxi in lieu of buses, there was little left to do but wait. She passed the time looking up things on the internet, with which she had a love/hate relationship. Fern preferred books, the dustier the better. The democratisation of information? She'd believe that when she saw it—few people seemed to do much of anything with the vast possibilities for knowledge it offered, preferring instead to sling insults at each other, perpetuate falsehoods, and indulge in banal exchanges. Still, she couldn't ignore its usefulness, so she regarded her small laptop and internet connection as sort of benign abominations, the result of a minor-league deal with the devil where she didn't so much sell her soul as lend it out from time to time.

In truth, the internet had for her personally been entirely a boon, putting her in touch with people at places like the Ghost Story Society, and on lists and forums where they could conduct civilised discussions about the work of writers like M.R. James, Oliver Onions, Walter de la Mare, and Vernon Lee. The internet had made it possible for her to obtain books with the click of a mouse rather than tracking down the names and addresses of used and antiquarian booksellers and conducting a laborious correspondence by mail as she'd done back in the 1990s. It had opened university archives to her. She was able to conduct her amateur scholarly research to a degree that would never have been possible in years past. But it was not in the way she would have chosen; for herself, she would have had what she imagined as the life of an academic in an earlier time, living at or near a university with hundreds of years of pedigree, spending most of her days researching rare and dusty tomes. She'd likely have needed to be a man as well, of course. She was aware that her ingratitude had far less to do with the internet itself than what it forever reminded her: that she had been born into the wrong time and place and family and body. Without it, in fact, she would have—and had when she was younger—almost no social contact at all, and certainly none that was meaningful. Online, she enjoyed a sizeable network of likeminded colleagues. Online she was inkblot, lowercase, sexless, and genderless, and she knew how she was perceived: as friendly, helpful, knowledgeable, reclusive, private. And that *was* the real Fern. In contrast, she had her drab office job with drab co-workers in her small drab Georgia town, and there was nothing real about that. She knew they all thought she was weird, and she didn't care. Why would she? How could she? In fact, she concealed the true reason for her trip, even the very destination, from her co-workers. How to explain to them that she was using the meagre vacation time they were permitted to visit an obscure village in England—even leaving the country would be unimaginable to them—in order to pursue a personal interest in a series of ghost stories broadcast on British television in the 1970s and based on the work of an early-twentieth century writer of supernatural fiction? Fortunately, Fern had cultivated a relationship among her co-workers of disinterested forbearance, and as it turned out, no one even asked her about where she was going or what she was going to do when she got there. No one cared.

England was both more and less than Fern could have imagined. It was more modern and vulgar but in other ways exactly as she had thought it would be. As the plane was circling for a landing, she pressed her face up against the window in amazement, staring at the patches of green below. "It's real, it's a real place," she thought, a thrill rising up through her body. All through the process of clearing immigration and customs and making her way across the airport she moved as in a dream, scarcely able to believe that all of her planning and saving had brought her here at last. Then there was the process of getting herself from the airport to Liverpool Street Station: a train, followed by the underground. Fern had never been on either a train or a subway before, and it was all she could do to keep herself from turning to the person next to her and exclaiming in delight. She had done her research, however, and knew the appropriate demeanour was one of stoicism. She would be stoic, then, even as her heart raced, even as she could not take her eyes off her fellow passengers. What a funny place the world was, that this could be the most mundane of journeys for them and one of the most exciting of her entire life.

What little she saw of London itself in this series of transfers left her aghast. So many different types of people, so much to see! Not just English people but women in burkhas and men in kurtas and fashionably dressed people and poorly dressed people and a cacophony of accents and language.

Her enthusiasm was undiluted by a small delay in her train's departure at Liverpool Street Station, where she passed the time with a latte and a croissant from a kiosk that appeared to be part of a chain—she was somewhat disappointed that something she envisioned as more distinctly English, a cup of tea and a scone perhaps, were not as readily in evidence, but perhaps in the villages it would be different. The ever-changing boards displaying departing train times and the lists of stations gave her a little stir. Part of her wanted to board a train at random and just travel forever, anonymous, lost, always moving.

At last, she passed through the barriers, boarded the train, and was away toward the Norfolk Coast. It was another uneventful journey, with one change, that again was, for Fern, suffused with excitement. And she had been awake for such a long time at that stage that she ought to have been exhausted, but she could no more conceive of sleeping than she could of bursting into song. She had intended to pass the first and longer train journey re-watching the 1972 "A Warning to the Curious" on her laptop, but instead she was unable to tear herself from the view outside the window. As the remnants of the city slipped away and they headed toward the coast and then north, she felt as she was slipping backward through time and space, slipping into the place that she ought to have been all along.

She had a brief changeover at Norwich with a second short train ride to North Walsham. The final leg of her journey was by taxi, and deposited her outside the pub where she had booked a room in the so-called signal box, a never-used structure built for a railway that did not exist. She was shown to her quarters by the friendly landlord and promised to be down shortly for a late lunch. She took a little time to look around the room, which had one double bed and a small single in the corner. A row of windows looked out over a beer garden and the sea beyond. Fern opened them in order to let in the sea air, and the curtains fluttered in the breeze. The room was reached by a steep set of steps, and when she sat on the bed, the opening to the staircase loomed a little menacingly. Someone or something could climb those stairs and if they did so quietly enough you would never know until they were almost upon you.

The next thing she knew she was waking on the double bed with the gloaming light outside. She was momentarily angry with herself—she had lost an entire precious afternoon, one of the few meaningful afternoons she would have in her life!—but anger gave way to reason; her body did need rest, after all, and she felt surprisingly renewed. She would wake at a reasonable hour the following day. She still had six full days remaining, after all. Her online friends had been unfailingly helpful in helping her design an itinerary that took in not just Happisburgh but Wells-next-the-Sea as well as Aldeburgh itself, which had served as the model for James's fictional Seaburgh.

Before that, though, Fern had another first in front of her: she would enter a pub alone, and dine there. Fern had never been to a pub before, alone or otherwise, or a bar, rather, for there were no such thing as pubs in the part of America that she came from. Sometimes her co-workers would meet up for happy hour at a chain restaurant like

Applebee's, but she always turned down their dutiful invitations, and she was sure they were as relieved as she was. The very idea made her shudder.

It all turned out to be much ado about nothing as the pub itself was only the tiny front room she'd already entered in order to be checked in, and she was in fact shown into the restaurant. Moreover, the pub clientele appeared to include families with children, dogs, and ladies decades her senior, so Fern found herself very comfortable as she took her chances with the alarming-sounding but in fact delicious suet pudding as her main dish. It wasn't a pudding at all but a kind of cross between a dumping and a pie with beef and gravy on the inside. She even grew so bold as to order a sherry with her meal. Fern was no drinker—she could count on one hand the number of times she had had an alcoholic beverage—but the jet-lag and the unfamiliar surroundings and the sheer excitement of everything had gone to her head, and sherry seemed like the sort of drink she might drink were she the scholarly gentleman of a different century she wished herself to be.

She was also a light eater, and so it was much to her surprise that she put away most of the heavy meal and even briefly contemplated dessert before making an even bolder decision: she would finish off the night with a glass of brandy by the fire in the pub. She knew the sherry had made her a little tipsy because she had to stifle a giggle as she ordered the brandy from the waitress, thinking: *I am ordering alcohol from books. The kinds of alcohol I think people in my books might order.*

Fern had never had two drinks in a row in her entire life, and it was with a growing sense of contentment and warmth that she sat by the fire sipping her brandy and watching the room glow and blur around her. In fact, it was some time before she became aware that someone had seated them-

74

selves in the chair across from her. It was an older gentle-man, well-dressed in an old-fashioned way, much to Fern's approval. He was saying something to her that she couldn't quite hear over the din of conversation around them.

"I beg your pardon?" she said, and he repeated, "How are you finding Happisburgh?"

For a moment she almost replied, "I found it on the internet" before realising what he meant, and she answered, "I just got here today, but it's really nice so far."

"Have you visited our churchyard yet? It's just next door, you know."

"I know," she said. "It's one of the things I came here to see." Her tongue felt thick, and she began to regret the brandy.

"Is it now! But you're an American?" The question was a mere courtesy; there was no way her accent could be mistaken. "How would you have found out about our little church?"

"I found it on the internet," she said at last, and regretted the brandy again. "I mean, from the BBC specials, actually," she explained. "The *Ghost Stories for Christmas*. I'm sort of a ghost story aficionado. M.R. James and all that."

The man broke into a smile. "Well, isn't that just—" He half turned in his seat as if to catch the attention of someone he remembered belatedly was no longer with him, and turned back to face her. "Isn't that just something," he said. "I knew I liked the look of you from the start. I'm a Jamesian myself, you know. Well, you don't know— how could you—but—well, at any rate, I'm pleased to make your acquaintance." He held out a hand and Fern reached out and took it. It occurred to her that this was the nic-est face to face conversation she had ever had in her life. She literally could not remember ever having met another person who shared her esoteric interests. "Look," the man went on, "I hope you don't think it's too forward of me, but would you like to accompany me to the churchyard now? The moon is nearly full and it's a beautiful evening."

Fern from back home would never have said yes; even Fern from earlier in the day would likely not have, but this was a new Fern, Fern with a bellyful of suet pudding and two alcoholic drinks. The next thing she knew, she and the gentleman, whose name was Mr. Ames and who supported himself with a cane (so surely he could not be any danger to her, Fern thought), were making their way across the gravel parking area in front of the pub to the churchyard just up the hill. They stood in front of the church, staring at the tower and the old gravestones all around and beyond, the sea.

"Look," said Mr. Ames, "look, look," and he pointed at the door of the church, above the door, "that's where the coat of arms was in 'A Warning to the Curious'. It wasn't real, of course, as you can see, or not see, as it is; they just added it for the show. The three crowns of the Kings of East Anglia! And here." He was pulling her across the churchyard. "Here is where Paxton found the grave of William Ager." There was nothing there, of course, that, too, had been an invention of the television show—it all had been an invention of Montague Rhodes James's imagination, she reminded herself. They straightened and looked out toward the sea just as Paxton had done. "Some of the graves are very old," said Mr. Ames. "Come back tomorrow in daylight. Do some rubbings if you like. Older than anything you have in America."

But she was barely listening to him, because now her imagination, or the alcohol and the jet-lag, were really playing tricks on her. "Do you see . . ." she started to say, and trailed off because it sounded so absurd she couldn't even form the words, and now it was gone—but no, she had seen it, and why shouldn't she have? A figure down on the shore. That she had been standing on the exact spot as Paxton when he saw the same, albeit more sinister, type of figure was nothing. This was a place people went on vacation, after all. And they did things like take walks on the beach. Especially on such a beautiful moonlit night.

She turned back to Mr. Ames, half expecting him to have vanished, but no, there he was, hale and hearty as before. "You'll be planning a visit to Wells-next-the-Sea then?" he said. "And what about Aldeburgh?"

"Yes," she said, "I've hired a taxi for tomorrow—" she liked the sound of that word *hired* in this context as it rolled off her tongue feeling foreign and strange and not-Fern yet so-very-Fern, like everything about this night, but Mr. Ames was having none of it.

"Nonsense! Nonsense!" he said, and he was almost shouting, so vehement was his protest. "I'll collect you myself in my car tomorrow and take you round." She protested; oh, no, she couldn't, couldn't think of imposing, but he would not be budged. Ten a.m. sharp, he'd be by, and she could look forward to being guided round by an expert.

It was only then she thought to look again, but the figure had vanished. Of course it had; the person had moved on, walking up the beach and out of her line of vision. She told herself that Mr. Ames's offer was very kind. She ignored the tiny swell of disappointment growing inside her that had been the pleasure of solitude, and of discovering things for herself.

She woke in a panic, not knowing where she was. It was not yet dawn. Of course: she was in England, on the Norfolk coast, and this was the signal box. There was nothing sinister about the yawning opening off to her left that was the steep set of stairs to the garden outside. Nor was there anything sinister about the sound of the wind and the surf, nor her pounding headache. That was definitely not sinister; that had the most prosaic explanation of all. The previous night, Fern had been quite drunk.

She was parched, and she got up and drank four glasses of water, one after the other, washing down four Advil with the final one. Then she drew a hot bath—there was no shower in the signal box—and lay down in it until the vise gripping her head loosened. By then the first streaks of dawn had appeared in the sky. It was still several hours before Mr. Ames was due to "collect" her, as he had said, and she thought she would steal some of the time to take a walk down on the beach before breakfast. If she remembered correctly, the beach sections of the story had been filmed at Wells-next-the-Sea, but from the beach here she was supposed to be able to see both the church and the iconic lighthouse.

Finding her way down to the beach proved a greater challenge than she had anticipated. There was what the English called a holiday caravan park on the other side of the pub, and she walked down to it thinking there must be a path to the beach from there. She found one, in the end, but it had been difficult to locate, and was even more difficult to navigate, a steep series of steps worn into the dirt cliff. An enterprising someone had helpfully added a rope that you could hang onto for additional leverage as you made your way down.

In Fern's experience, beaches meant blazing heat, white sands, blue water, and a lot of the kind of people she would cross the street to avoid. She knew other types of beaches existed but had never seen one until this moment. Suddenly the beaches she knew in America seemed so eager to please. This beach did not care about anyone. It simply was, a wild stretch of sand and a pounding surf that was tearing away at the land at an alarming rate. The coastline that she was seeing here would be very different from the one M.R. James would have been familiar with although even then the erosion had been a problem: "The sea has encroached tremendously, as you know, all along that bit of coast," one character had said to Professor Parkins in "Oh, Whistle, and I'll Come to You, My Lad".

The beach was marred by ugly industrial skeletal structures that must have been erected to stop erosion but she could not imagine how, or how the eyesore they created and the way they made the beach almost entirely unusable could be an improvement on the natural forces they were attempting to hold at bay. Further up, though, the beach was mercifully free of them. She could indeed see the church tower as well as the lighthouse from here, and as she walked further up the beach she came to another break in the cliffs, this a wide and easy if steep path that led up to a parking area. The lighthouse was just to her left. Paxton had cycled past it in "A Warning to the Curious".

She followed the road leading up from the parking area, reasoning that it might take her back toward the pub more efficiently as the morning was already passing rapidly. Her instinct had been correct, and she made it back to the pub in time for breakfast. As the owner served her an ample meal, she inquired about the structures she'd seen and was informed that they had been built in the 1950s. The elements had had their way with them, however, and they had failed to significantly slow the erosion and had eventually been abandoned. This whole area had been abandoned to the sea, she thought, and wondered how long this pub would be here.

She had a few moments of hoping Mr. Ames would not turn up after all, but turn up he did, and off they went to explore the Jamesian country of the Norfolk coast.

They had a pleasant enough day together. In fact, if someone had described it to Fern as a day that had belonged to her that she could not remember, she would have imagined it to have been one of the best days of her life. Not only was she spending it with someone who "got" her passions to a degree no one ever had before, but she was visiting places she had only ever dreamed of. They drove an hour north along the coast to Wells-next-the-Sea, where the pine forest stretched down to the beach, and wandered in search of the hill where the third crown of the Anglo-Saxon kings was buried—and where the unfortunate Paxton met his terrible fate. "We won't be doing any digging today!" Mr. Ames shouted heartily, and she laughed even though it wasn't funny.

Then they went south to Waxham where they walked along the same stretch of coast on which Professor Parkin had discovered the cursed whistle in the TV adaptation. Mr. Ames had wanted to continue to Aldeburgh, but she pointed out it was growing far too late. Besides, she had booked two nights in Aldeburgh at the end of the week—at what James had called "The Bear" and what was today The White Lion—so there was no point in driving all the way there before then.

At the end of it all she was exhausted, not exhilarated, and despite reassuring him she would be okay on her own, Mr. Ames insisted on monopolising her company into the evening. He took his dinner nightly at the pub where she was staying, he told her, and they would have dinner together there and talk about the day they'd had. He would hear of nothing else.

Eventually she couldn't bear the sound of his voice any longer. She put her fork down, said sorry but she was feeling ill, and escaped to the signal box.

Fern shut the door behind her and stood for a moment with her eyes closed, savouring the solitude and the relative quiet. Then she began to climb the steep set of steps to her room, only halfway up she hesitated. Did she hear something coming from the room? Was someone else in there? She bounded up the final few steps as if to catch them in the act, as if there was some other way by which the person could escape if she was not fast enough, although of course that was not the case. But the room was empty, and exactly as she left it: windows open and curtains fluttering, her little suitcase with the lid up on the single bed, her books and papers scattered about as she had left them. The sound of people laughing and talking in the beer garden below drifted up. Fern sat down on the edge of her bed and suddenly, much to her surprise, she began to cry.

She thought at first that she did not know why, but of course she did. She cried because the day she had so painstakingly planned for so long had been hijacked by this man who, however nice he was, was also astonishingly overbearing. Only then did it occur to her that she had been taken under the wing of one of James's avuncular characters. It would have been funny were it not so upsetting. But she cried for other reasons as well: because it was the end of another day, and each day that ended brought her closer to her inevitable return to her normal life—and what then? What would she have to look forward to? It had taken her years to save up for this trip; would she begin saving up again? Would her life be nothing but years of frugality punctuated by a few days of truly living, only for it all to come to a close too soon and the drudgery of work to begin again? Fern wept for the life she could not have, would never have, could not have had, because she had been born into the wrong time and place, or maybe because it was a life that had never existed for anyone outside of books.

It almost would have been better if she had never come here.

For the first time in her life since she was a child, Fern cried herself to sleep.

She woke in the middle of the night. She felt calm and emptied out. She rose and went to the window and the moon was high and the surf was pounding the land. She scoured the beach for dark figures, lurking, beckoning or menacing her, but she saw no one.

In the morning she thought it was so dull it might have been a dream.

A message was waiting for her at breakfast. Mr. Ames was so sorry that she had taken ill the previous night. He hoped that she was feeling better, and he would be round to collect her again at ten for more adventures.

Fern felt her temper rise as she gazed down at the note. How dare he, she thought. "How dare he," she whispered out loud, and saying it felt good. How dare he insinuate himself into her life, into her solitude. How dare he take over her vacation in this way.

She was waiting for him outside in the pebbled parking area when he pulled in. She did not even wait for him to stop the car and get out; she went to his window.

"I'd rather be alone today," she said.

Of course, he asked about the following day, and the day after that. He made her say it. "Look," she said, "you're very kind, but I just prefer to be on my own. I wanted to spend these days here on my own."

She told herself it was not a look of hurt and confusion that crossed his face. She told herself that she had done nothing wrong. She was right to assert herself.

After he drove away, she phoned and rebooked the cab she'd had to cancel the previous morning. In time, the man turned up, mildy resentful about the abrupt change of plans the day before, but somewhat mollified at having her business returned, and she had him drive her round to the same locations she'd visited with Mr. Ames. She tried to pretend that day had not happened, as though she were experiencing it all for the first time.

It was all for nought. The places were tainted now. They weren't hers. That was it: she had hoped to come here and make something hers, for once, and it felt like that had been taken from her.

That night she went to dinner in the pub, and of course Mr. Ames was there. They nodded to one another cordially and stiffly, like old acquaintances who had fallen out with one another. This, then, was spoiled as well. Fern opted for a salmon fillet that she only picked at and finally gave up on. She went back to her room to read and perhaps watch another of the ghost stories. She told herself that the next day would be different; this one had been marred by her difficult encounter with Mr. Ames at the start of it.

But as she lay in the flickering light of "Oh, Whistle, and I'll Come to You, My Lad", she could not stop an incessant thought from ratcheting around in her brain: that she had only four days left. Four days and then it was back to the airport from Aldeburgh on Saturday, back to her dreary life. She hated this train of thought; she hated that now she was here, she couldn't even properly *be* here, couldn't stop thinking of what she was going back to. Live in the moment, in the now; it was the sort of thing said by people Fern thought of as soppy-headed and irritating, but they had a point. If only she could. "Who is this," murmured Professor Parkin on her tinny laptop speakers, "who is coming?" *It is I*, thought Fern. *I am coming.* And she also thought: *I long for something extraordinary like this to happen to me. To find a cursed whistle or the crown of an Anglo-Saxon king. Even if it did bring death and horror in its wake. Even then. Because that would be something significant at least.*

Fed up, Fern shoved her laptop away, shutting its lid. If she was so anxious about losing time, why was she tucked up here in her room like this, doing what she could do every night when she was home? And why should she let that awful Mr. Ames—no, not awful, she reminded herself, just overbearing—force her into hiding like this? She had as much right to be out and about as he did.

Fern took herself back down to the pub. Although she didn't particularly want more alcohol—memories of her painful hangover lingered—she went boldly to the bar and ordered a brandy. Mr. Ames was nowhere to be seen. She returned to the same spot by the fire she had occupied two nights earlier, and she sat and sipped her drink. Try as she might, it was impossible to summon up the feelings she'd had on the first night. She supposed that she had been counting on this trip to transform her in some way. She was not transformed at all. She was still Fern Blackwell; she didn't even feel like inkblot, her internet persona. She felt drab and perpetually disappointed that as ever, nothing was turning out the way it should.

Fern was furious. She knocked back the brandy like she'd seen people do in films, and she left the pub and headed back toward the caravan park. She didn't have a flashlight, but once again, the moon was high and bright and lit her way. From the cliff with the steps cut into it she could see that the tide was low, and out far. She descended down toward the sea and began walking up the shore.

"It's a real night for walking on the water," she said to herself, just as Doctor Black had to Paxton, but no figure appeared as had subsequently happened in the film. She thought how strange it was, the way movies were made, cobbling together locations like these to create some entirely new place, a place that might not exist in the same way that Happisburgh or Wells-next-the-Sea did, but had nonetheless been brought into being. She felt as if she were just on the verge of finding that place, as though she could peel back the veil if only she could work out just the right place to stand or just the right way to look at things. In books, people always had to say certain words in a certain way, or hold a talisman. She had none of those things, only her will. And in the end, in real life, people's wills didn't amount to much.

She realised she was cold, and she had not dressed warmly enough for the walk. She thought of turning back but reckoned she was midpoint between the cliff path and the road that would take her back, so she might as well carry on in the direction she was going. The wind was biting. She pressed on down the beach. She thought of the strange coastline at Wells-next-the-Sea, with the pine forest stretching right down to the beach. She turned and scanned the horizon behind her, half-hoping to see a hooded figure in pursuit, but there was only the sand, the sea, and the night sky above. The sea was as black as the sky, and you could mix them up, fall into either, and drown. If I drowned, Fern thought, I would never have to go back. I could stay here. In a thousand years, archaeologists might uncover my bones. Or I'd be lost forever in the sand and the silt and the sea. Both options seemed equally appealing, and far more tempting than the idea of getting on a plane at the end of the week and returning to her old life.

Fern found herself growing angry. "You were supposed to change me," she said out loud to the sea, to the place. Nothing out here cared. She was an interloper, and the place knew it in its ancient bones. It did not have to share its wonders and terrors with her.

She had made her way to the other end of the beach, and the steep path leading up to the car park. *Who is this who is coming?* It's only me, only Fern. She felt like a ghost herself, only a ghost that everyone was indifferent to. Maybe that was what led to people becoming ghosts after they died: not great suffering, or earthly ties, but indignation. Fury that one was ignored in life made the dead determined that they would be noticed before moving on to the afterlife. If she could not become a scholar of antiquarian books, perhaps being a terrifying apparition was the next best thing.

At the top of the path, she turned and looked at the stretch of sand and sea and then at the flat meadows leading to the lighthouse. She imagined a spectre moving across it toward her. It would have terrible twig-like hands reaching for her. In place of a head there would be only a skull with a few wisps of hair still stuck to it as a horrible reminder that it had, once, been alive—just as she now was. Its mouth would be locked in that eternal skull-grin. Would it speak? She decided that it would, but would its voice be hoarse and guttural like a demon or would it be reedy like a ghost?

A chill ran up her spine and she actually shuddered; she had succeeding in spooking herself, almost without realising what she was doing. A cloud passed in front of the moon, and Fern soon wished that the night was not so dark. She began walking toward the road that she knew would lead her back toward the village and to the pub and the signal box. Without the moon, she could see only a few feet in front of her, yet surely it was impossible to get lost. There was only the one road, after all.

It was so very quiet that she could hear the sound of her own footfalls. They were a kind of comfort to her, until she stopped for a moment and realised that her footsteps did not. Her heart fluttered for a moment, and then she smiled: someone else was with her on this suddenly-moonless night. "Hello?" she called out expectantly.

The footfalls stopped for a moment, and what she heard

then was a sound she could never have described. It was neither of the silly voices she had just imagined, the guttural demon-voice or the soft whisper of a ghost, but all the same, it reminded her of nothing more than the grave. It was a sound that was full of dead things, one that had rotted and choked on worms.

It did not speak—it did nothing more than take a breath—but that single impossible intake of breath rent a hole in the fabric of the world, that breath of a dead thing. *A dead thing; a dread thing*, Fern thought, and she tried to speak again but she could not. She thought, *I brought you into being, but I did not mean it. I did not mean it!* She heard it breathe again, and she knew then that it was trying to say something: *Who. Who is. Who is thisssss.*

Fern could not run. She was frozen like an animal, as though stillness could save her. Now it was before her. It was thin and wrapped in a grave shroud that flapped in the wind. Its eyes were empty sockets that still saw. On its skull flapped ruined bits of flesh and long stringy black hairs, a kind of memento mori: *I was once as you are, you will one day become as I am.* It smelled of something ancient that had been underground for a very long time, and had gone mad down there. A coldness descended upon her, and she found her voice at last. "I did not mean it," she whispered. The sound of her own voice gave her strength. "I did not mean it," she said again, and then she was shouting even as it bore down on her: "I did not—I did not ask for it! I did not mean it! You must go away from me! You must!"

No one saw the strange American woman over the next two days. The landlord, his wife, and Mr. Ames all noticed her absence, and remarked upon it, but as she had booked until Wednesday, it was outside their remit to disturb her if she did not wish to be disturbed. However, the day of her scheduled departure came and still she did not appear. It was necessary to ready the room for the next guests, and so at last the landlord took it upon himself to enter.

What he found inside was a room in utter disarray. The bedclothes, the pillows, all had been thrown about, as had her things: clothing, notebooks, papers. But Miss Blackwell herself was nowhere to be found. There was a strong odour of the sea about the room, not the healthy scent of the sea air but the rotting smell of decaying fish and dead seaweed, yet although they stripped the beds and looked everywhere, they could not discover its source, and within a few hours of the discovery it had dissipated entirely. They packed up Miss Blackwell's things and considered what they ought to do: notify authorities first, perhaps, then try to reach someone related to her back in the States? But might those things only make more trouble for what had seemed a very troubled woman? In the end, they settled for putting her things away in a back room and sending her an email. She did not reply, but they had not really expected her to anyway. After some time the entire incident actually receded from their memory, as often happens with events that cannot be reconciled with any sort of linear apprehension of reality. Guests from time to time began to report a troubled night's sleep in the signal box, and on more than one occasion they asked to be moved, or left altogether without even quarrelling about a refund. When many months later the landlord thought to look again at Miss Blackwell's belongings, reasoning that at that stage she was unlikely to ever return and demand them back, they were nowhere to be found. He concluded that his wife must have disposed of them in some way, but he did not think to ever ask her about their fate, and they never spoke of her again.

The Queen in the Yellow Wallpaper

We have come to Carcosa. That's the name, anyway, that my partner's sister gave to this house, in some flight of fancy back when she was still well. Or so we thought. I suppose even at that stage she might have been—might have been what? "Starting her descent into madness" sounds so very Gothic; nowadays we use words like "bipolar" and "major depressive disorder" to make it sound like those episodes are mere maladies which require only a proper course of treatment to set their sufferers on the path to a cure. And yet what bedevils Sarah seems not so much a disease of the mind or body as it is a sickness of her soul—and I don't believe in the soul. But for as long as I've known her, for the dozen years that Adam and I have been together, there's been a kind of shadow over Sarah. The rest of the family is happy-go-lucky, even annoyingly so—as though Sarah has always taken on the burden of sorrow for the rest of them. But—you see—Sarah's peripatetic habits of mind seem already a creeping influence on me here. I don't work as a scientist, but I'm trained as one, and it isn't like me to indulge in these sorts of whims. It's the middle of the night here and I'm tired and stressed out—and in this state I'm no help to Adam *or* Sarah.

In the middle of the night, my imaginings get the better of me. My fears take shape and peel themselves from the ugly yellow wallpaper someone's maligned the walls with and they stalk the corridors of Carcosa. They ooze like ectoplasm round my thoughts to fog my brain.

More tomorrow, when I'm feeling myself again.

So. First things first. We have come here, Adam and I, to look after his older sister Sarah. Or rather Adam has come to look after Sarah and I have come because, because—because I go where Adam goes? That doesn't sound right somehow. That is not what I ever intended. And yet it has become the way.

It came upon us gradually, as these things do, this intertwining; there were the career goals that clashed, practically and geographically; late nights and tears, a counsellor to talk us through it all because we are responsible middle-class people who don't give up on a marriage without a fight, and in the end a capitulation on my part. Did I say capitulation? I mean compromise, of course. My dream was the more impractical of the two, given the circumstances. Not impossible, not even unrealistic, but certainly impractical in a modern world where two modern people both want certain things. Does it matter, specifically, the substance of our competing goals? In the end, I think not; it's an ordinary story, lived daily in millions of ordinary lives. Adam won, I lost, life goes on.

But in the end this capitulation has left me dependent on Adam. Not utterly, and Adam would blanch at my use of the word "dependent". He sees us as *interdependent*, maybe *symbiotic*, perhaps tethered—no, not tethered, that implies two, and Adam resolutely wants us to be as one. If we are one, then nobody has won and nobody has lost.

And yet here is another capitulation, albeit a smaller one: while Adam was granted a leave of absence to take care of this full-fledged family emergency, I had to quit my job to come here to Carcosa. I didn't like my job; it's not what I trained to do or ever imagined doing. I was little more than a glorified receptionist in an office surrounded by people all doing much more important things than me, but it was something. It was mine.

There was never any question of my staying behind. We must remain a united front. It's why people cleave to one another; it's what we do; it's our way of ensuring we are never alone in the dark.

It's strange for me because Sarah and I have never been close. Sarah is the sort of woman who makes me feel uncomfortable, to be honest. She's very intense, in that New York City artist sort of way. In fact, a New York City artist is exactly what she is: a playwright, and a rather good one from all accounts. I say *from all accounts* because experimental and avant garde theatre is far from my forte; I have attended a couple of performances of Sarah's plays and came away baffled and a little bit disturbed. One appeared to be the tale of an erotic triangle between a woman (also played by Sarah), a dwarf, and a—here I admit I don't know what it was. I'm not even sure it was human. I think they were living on the edge of a cliff. I think the cliff was symbolic of something. You see? I have no idea what I was watching, but it was the sort of thing people describe afterward as "challenging". One reviewer wrote it "invented and then smashed new paradigms", whatever that means.

She is working on another play now. It's mostly what she does all day, every day, holed up in her room. I am not sure it's good for her. I think it may be feeding her depression or whatever it is she's going through, but Adam says it's good for her to have work to do.

Sarah has strong features and a severe black bob and she doesn't smile very easily. She's attractive, but attractive like an elaborate and expensive piece of jewellery, all glitter and sharp edges.

She has, from what Adam tells me, always suffered from depressions and malaises and manic periods, but none of that ever seemed unmanageable until Carcosa.

Now. Carcosa. I have not even begun to describe *you*.

Carcosa is a sprawling heap of a house. It is the house of my bookish childhood fantasies. You know the sort. Old and rambling and surely possessed of hidden doors and passageways and gruesome secrets.

It's an odd colour, coated in a sort of sickly yellow-green paint. From its once-grand but now-sagging front steps and porch to its two actual turrets thrusting out from the house at the front—into which it is unsafe to walk, as rainwater has leaked through the roofs for years and rotted their flooring—it's in desperate need of money and attention, of which Sarah has neither. How she came into possession of the place is peculiarly Gothic as well; she was married, for a short time, to a man whom none of the family knew well and Adam and I never even met. They decamped from her cramped Williamsburg apartment to his ancestral home here, and then, quite suddenly, he died. He had no family at all, and the house passed to her.

The house is old, its foundations and inner rooms dating back to colonial times. Each generation that came into possession of it made additions and architectural embellishments and what stands today is a sort of hideous discordant symphony of a house. If one can believe Sarah's accounts (and that's a big *if*) and *if* you believe in this sort of thing

(Adam and I do not), it was passed around between rich and decadent artistic and occult dilettantes, inciting the usual sorts of rumours of shocking activities, sacrifice, and summons to supernatural entities. There was at some stage round the turn of the twentieth century a rather grand week-long affair that ended in many of the participants' breakdowns, and there may have been a crime committed—when she comes to this part, Sarah is more than usually reticent. I imagine the spectre of this madness has infected the walls and seeped into the floorboards and lingers in the very air we are breathing.

This is all I know about Carcosa.

The backyard is crawling with tangles of thorn and brush, and infested by biting insects; the front is overgrown as well, but only with weeds and grass. Adam keeps saying we must look for a mower on the premises but he never does.

The yard is enormous. The house is enormous. I keep trying to count how many rooms it actually contains and losing track. Plus there are little areas within rooms, alcoves set apart by steps going up or down or, in at least one case, rotting curtains dividing one area from the other (I say *at least one case* because I have trouble keeping the rooms straight and sometimes I count them more than once), and I cannot decide whether these are separate rooms or not. If I didn't know any better, I would think someone was creeping into the house at night and rearranging the rooms to trick us.

It is a house that ought to be allowed to disintegrate quietly into its own memory and ruin.

It's an unhealthy house. Let me rephrase that: it seems to be an unhealthy atmosphere for Sarah, which is not to say that the house *itself* is unhealthy; that's a bit of a bizarre anthropomorphism, isn't it? It is not what I meant to say. I have told Adam that I think it's best if he works toward getting Sarah into a different environment; even once she's well, I think she would do better in an apartment in town. Anybody would.

It seems to me that the worst excesses of Carcosa would prey upon even the strongest and healthiest minds, let alone one already wracked by illness like sister Sarah.

I told Adam this after he came to bed last night—late, because Sarah has been having crying fits, and sometimes he's afraid to leave her alone—but he didn't say anything back to me at all.

I knew that this would be challenging, but it's proving to be more difficult than I ever imagined.

There is not really an end date for our time here. It seems mad to say that this did not occur to me, but it didn't. We didn't set out from our nice suburban Massachusetts home into the countryside as though we were embarking on some long journey. We didn't batten the hatches—we didn't even pack much of our stuff—we were careless in bidding our friends goodbye. I'll catch up with them online, I thought, and see them in a few weeks.

It never occurred to me that there would be no *online* in Carcosa. Even were one to run cables under the earth or launch a satellite to catch a passing signal, I feel sure the house itself would strangle the transmission. Our phones don't work here, either. It feels eerie, like we are trapped in one of those stories where we're already dead and don't yet realise it. Adam thinks our isolation is wonderful. He points out that Sarah has a landline installed, so can't I still phone someone if I'm feeling lonely, and it isn't as though we can't take the car and go into town when we need a break. In the meantime, he says, isn't it nice to be away from *all that*?

I don't know what he means by *all that*, and even though he says we can go into town any time, we never do. Adam is afraid to leave Sarah on her own, so I've taken the car out a few times for a drive. But there's not really a "town" to go into anyway, just a series of winding rural roads that eventually give way to a grim main street lined with closed or failing businesses. I suppose this place must have been prosperous a hundred years ago. Anyway, I worried about getting lost, and the GPS was acting up, and it just didn't seem worth the trip and the fretting anyway. In town, there wasn't even a café to stop off at for a cup of coffee.

I did visit the grocery store, and the bright lights shocked me—I had not realised Carcosa is swathed in a kind of perpetual gloom. At the store, people laughed and talked loudly, spoke into their phones, wrangled their disruptive children. I revelled in it. I said to the man at the meat counter that the steaks looked nice and I bought three of them, one for each of us, and I chatted with a woman by the freezer about the weather we'd been having—Weather? At Carcosa, I hardly notice weather—and the cashier and I commiserated about the price of gas these days. As I pushed my cart across the parking lot I felt almost light-hearted, and I recognised this feeling as one I used to call *ordinary*.

Back at Carcosa, I tried to speak to Adam about how long we'll be staying here, and he laughed at my concern. He said I was being dramatic. He said we were just getting Sarah stabilised, didn't I remember that she sometimes had these episodes and once we got her into a pattern of taking her meds again, once we got her past this rough patch, everything would be fine.

Fine, I wanted to say. *Leaving a mentally ill woman here at Carcosa sounds fine to you?* But I didn't say that. I said, *This rough patch, how long does it last?*

And he laughed again and said even doctors can't answer a question like that, now, can they, and then he went on his way, like we'd just had an actual satisfactory conversation with a resolution and everything, and I sat in the living room? parlour? sitting room?—as I've said, this house has so many rooms, and it's not really clear what the purpose for most of them is—and wondered just how that talk had gone so badly. I had even tried using some of the techniques that the counsellor had taught us years ago: when you do *x*, I feel *y*. It didn't seem to work. I thought those things would work.

I just thought things would work better.

So we've been here ten days now. It seems like longer. It seems like my whole life I've been opening my eyes to the lumpy yellow ceiling that is above our bed in Carcosa, and that each day will begin in this way for the rest of my life.

I don't know what Adam does with his time, with his days. Sometimes I go hours without seeing him. He spends time with Sarah, of course. I try to do so as well, but my presence seems to upset her. She showed me a few pages of the play at one stage, out of order, and I couldn't make heads or tails of them and that made her angry. I want to be a help for both of them, but it seems the best way I can do that is to be as invisible as possible and do things that are needed: making sandwiches for everyone's lunches, that sort of thing.

These little tasks don't take me very long, so I have had to find other things to interest me.

I have become particularly interested in the north turret.

That I cannot step into it, across its threshold, because it is dangerous—I find this so compelling. I *want* to step into it. I feel like it's taunting me, this turret. This is the one from which I always imagine I hear the footsteps, the dragging noises. That's my overactive imagination, of course. There's a bad smell coming from it, *not* my imagination, because at some stage some ill-advised person put down carpet, and the carpet is rotting. The carpet is a sort of burnt orange and it clashes with the unpleasant yellow wallpaper. Possibly this was fashionable in the 1970s, which was probably the last time anyone put any money into the place. Today the effect is not fashionable but horrific. A fashion crime!

I am trying to be flippant. There's no flippancy in this house, no humour. Even that word I wrote, *crime*, I'm looking at it and it's taking on sinister aspects: *three isolated people alone in a country home and one's thoughts turn to . . . murder!*

Such is the power of Carcosa, you know.

Today Adam came across me there, sitting on the floor just outside the turret. He startled me; I had not heard anyone stirring in the house for hours. I felt his appearance had spoiled something. You see, I have this fanciful notion about the north turret. I imagine that if I were to cross the threshold, I would step not into the foul-carpeted, floorboard-rotted, ugly-wallpapered turret, but into another reality—another world, like a children's story where they walk through a door in a wall into another land.

And I suppose there is a part of me that wants to step out of this place and into another world, one where—

Well. One where everything is different.

Adam said, "What are you doing here? I've been looking all over for you."

I said, "I've been right here the whole time. Adam, do you think this turret has changed?"

"Changed how? From the rest of the house? It's certainly uglier."

"Changed from how it was yesterday, and the day before that."

"That sounds like something out of one of Sarah's plays. Maybe it's catching," Adam said, and we waited there for a little while longer watching the turret room, just in case, but it stayed the same and so did we.

Tonight I cooked the steaks I'd bought us in town. I thought it would be a nice treat, but Adam came in the kitchen looking at me like I was crazy and asked me what I was doing. I said I thought I was making dinner.

"What the hell?" he said. "You know Sarah's a vegetarian."

I do know that Sarah's a vegetarian. I know this very well and I stared at the steaks sizzling in the pan, very good steaks, nice marbled cuts I'd planned to serve up rare and succulent, and I wondered what hell I'd been thinking before Adam even got around to asking that as a follow up question.

I said, "I don't know what I was thinking. I guess I wasn't. Look, I'll fix her a salad or something."

You see, though. It's little things like that, insignificant maybe, that make me feel like I'm not myself. And I imagine it's the place, Carcosa, exerting its influence and turning my own mind shaky and unfamiliar. If being here is having this effect on me, what must it do to Sarah?

Then Adam said he thinks the play Sarah is writing is upsetting her. That he wants her to stop working on it but he doesn't know how to make her stop.

Has he tried asking her? I want to know.

I would describe the look he gave me as "withering". Of course; he has requested, he has demanded, he has cajoled, he has even shouted. All to no avail. Sarah goes on writing.

We talk some more. I take the steaks out to rest. I finally begin to get a sense of what Adam is doing all day.

It's the damn play.

When they were children Sarah had bossed him around; she'd scribble down stories and force him to act all the parts, and this time, it seems, things are no different. She is working very hard on this particular play, and seems very determined.

I asked him what the play is about, and he had a hard time describing it to me. He said it was about a woman isolated in a strange house in the country, and I said like this place, and he looked startled and said no, not like this place at all. It's different, very different, but he couldn't say how.

He said that the woman in the play was in a house because people had forced her to stay there. I asked what people and he shook his head and said that wasn't really an important part of the story, but the way he said it made me feel like it might be the most important part and he just didn't want to talk about it. He seemed shaken. Then, he said, a queen arrived.

"At the house?" I said. "In the middle of nowhere? The queen of what?"

Adam said, "A terrible queen. Her presence drives people to madness."

That doesn't sound like the healthiest subject matter for my sister-in-law, does it? I said so to Adam.

"She wants to talk with you," he said. "She wants your opinion of the play."

"My opinion . . . ?" What do I know about that sort of thing?

"It doesn't matter what you tell her," Adam said. Doesn't it? Sarah isn't an idiot or a child. What are we doing here, anyway? I thought we came here to offer a bit of familial support, not a full program of medical assistance like we're staff in an institution. Anyway, maybe Sarah needs to go

to one of those institutions for a while. Or whatever it is
they call them now—I guess they just say people are hos-
pitalised. Who was her doctor, anyway? Shouldn't she be
seeing someone regularly?

I said I would talk to her after dinner, but I didn't want
to eat steak any longer. I wrapped up two of them and put
them in the fridge while Adam wolfed his down; I threw
some lettuce and tomatoes into a bowl and called it a salad.
And now I am sitting alone in the kitchen with my notebook and the salad, making up excuses in my head for all
the reasons I don't want to go to Sarah's room.

Her room is down a long corridor on the ground floor, with
two sets of three steps each taking you down to a lower level.

I knocked on the door, and she opened it. I hadn't seen
her in days. Her eyes were bright, eager, and feverish. I was
struck by how thin she seemed. Sarah's always been birdlike
in build but this is something more, as though there's simply
no substantial meat left on her bones at all. Her normally
severe black bob was uncombed and unsevere.

"I'm so glad you came," Sarah said, like I was a neighbour
paying her a social call. She put her hand on my free wrist,
the one not holding the sad excuse for a salad; she felt dry
and fragile and hot.

I held the salad out in front of me like a shield.

"I made you dinner," I said.

"Oh, thank you," Sarah said, and took it from me without looking at it and set it aside. I took a moment to look
around the room. It had that smell about it of a closed-up
place where someone has been spending too much time; it
was disarrayed, covered in Sarah's clothing and papers that
had things scribbled and crossed out on them. "Sit here,"

Sarah said, retreating to the edge of an unmade wrought iron single bed. I sat beside her. She rummaged under the bedclothes and pulled out a stack of papers and thrust them at me. "Tell me what you think," she demanded.

"Oh, Sarah, I'm hardly qualified—"

"Just do it," she said. "Adam can't understand. It's not for him, you know. For men. It's a play for women. About what they do to us."

I said, "I really don't—"

"Read it out loud," she said. "It's the only way to read a play. Do it now."

I did as she told me. At the time I was thinking that the easiest way to get out of there was to do as she asked, and I felt quite determined that as soon as I left I was going to talk to Adam. There was nothing more we could do for Sarah here. She needed more help than we could give.

But I began to read the play, and though it was only words on a page, a strange emotion overtook me. I can only describe the reading of it as being akin to listening to a powerful piece of music. It moved me in the same way that songs can capture your emotions so primally, the way they can gut you, the way they have a rhythm and a life to them.

The play felt like a spell.

The reason that Adam had been unable to describe it to me is that the events that unfold in it are the least of it. Everything in the play is a vehicle for the intoxicated words that Sarah must have scribbled during all-night manias; they made me feel manic but exhilarated as well. And the characters—there are more of them than I expected, from what Adam had said in describing the main character as *isolated* and I found myself wondering if they had somehow not made an appearance for him—and the characters kept saying to one another *the queen, the queen is coming*, and whenever they did so I felt a shudder of pleasure and anticipation so intense I could scarcely keep myself from crying out.

It is savage. The play is a savage thing.

Of course, I recognised the setting as Carcosa, and how stupid Adam was not to have done so immediately. Tears pricked my eyes as I set down the last page and turned to Sarah, sitting next to me on the bed. "When will she be here?" I asked her. "The queen, I mean."

She smiled at me and said, "It won't be long now at all."

"I meant in the play," or did I? I was starting to feel confused. Had I not, too, dreamed of the arrival of the queen?

A shadowy figure stepping out of the turret room. Royal robes made of skin and memory and deceit. Beauty from rot. All Carcosa would be transformed when she walked among us at last.

I've just read what I've written here. That last bit above. It isn't like me. It isn't me. I knew this was a bad place. I don't believe in the things I'm writing about here. There must be some explanation; some poison in the house seeping into our brains and changing our thoughts. The place ought to be inspected for that kind of thing, and probably torn down. But that is later. For the present I must find Adam and persuade him to leave, that we must all leave.

I am ashamed to write what happened next with Sarah. Adam, of course, must never know. If she tells him I shall feign ignorance; I will remind him of her madness. She said she was the queen's proxy, and I believed her. When she kissed me it was the most beautiful and terrible secret thing. Later I woke and didn't know where I was. Sarah was still asleep next to me and for many dreadful seconds I didn't recognise her. I dressed as quietly and quickly as I could and hurried out of the room and I have since been searching for Adam and he is nowhere to be seen and I am so frightened, frightened without reason and no one to tell and feeling that if I write it all down I will make sense of it soon.

I am going to burn these pages shortly.

It is dusk. I am outside the turret room again. I have been here for some time. I don't know how long, but I have seen the sun pass through the sky at least twice or perhaps thrice.

Sarah looks after me. She brings me water and a little food, but I only drink, I don't eat. I want to be as pure as possible for the arrival of the queen.

I don't know where Adam is spending his days any longer. I saw him once from the window, but I cannot understand how he made his way so deep into the thickets of the backyard. He may be lost out there for all I know, but Sarah says it's nothing to concern myself with, even though he appears to have stripped himself naked at some point, for I can see bits of his tattered clothing stuck to brambles and flapping forlornly in the wind that is kicking up all around Carcosa. It's been blowing very hard for a while now, maybe hours, maybe days. It's hard to tell. I don't remember when I began to lose track of the time. That's funny, isn't it? Because if I knew, that would mean I hadn't lost track, wouldn't it?

I don't remember because it doesn't matter. Because *she* will be with us soon and when she is here all that is will collapse into ruin just like Carcosa. Sarah has been so very hard at work writing her into reality, drawing her into being.

The wind is howling at us like a living thing. I can't tell if it is on our side or not. Sarah keeps coming in and reciting new lines and when she does the wind screams louder, nearly drowning her voice. She reads these words to me: "And something wakes in the darkness and wakes in the air and wakes in my bones and we wait for our goddess, our ruler of Carcosa, our charnel queen."

Something stirs in the turret, something long asleep, something stretching, something starting to be.

And we gaze into her shadows, into her bleak beauty, into her nothingness, into her void. She is the hollowness that haunts us all, she is the abyss, she is the dark beyond the dark and the emptiness of collapsing stars, and she draws us into her sweet embrace.

The Wife's Lament

Ful oft wit beotedan
þæt unc ne gedælde   nemne deað ana
owiht ells;   eft is þæt onhworfen
is nu   fornumen swa hit no wære
freondscipe uncer.

We two often vowed
that death alone would separate the two of us
nothing else; now that is changed
it is now as though it never was,
our love.

– Anonymous Old English Lyric

I n the beginning, Penny loved everything, and as time
went on, she grew to loathe it all.

First, the cold that might creep up at any time of year,
even at the height of July or August: an aching, draining,
damp, enduring chill, and you couldn't run the heat for
long anyway because of the cost of heat, and the houses all
seemed to be built wrong, as though designed by people
who didn't know they were making houses for cold, damp,
miserable climates. Next, the cost of everything that *wasn't*
heating, from sweaters (jumpers) to takeout (takeaway) to
gas (petrol) for their car. Ian was neither stingy nor poor,
but she couldn't help noticing the prices of things all the
same, and fretting over it, even as people admonished her

that she had to stop converting everything to dollars in her head. Third, the loud and public drunks who spilled out from the late-night pub up the street on weekends, vomiting in their front yard (garden) often as not, shouting abuse at one another as they reeled up the sidewalk (pavement).

Then her dislikes became wholly irrational, and she knew it, and hated herself for it and went on disliking things anyway: the youth, hanging about at bus stops and outside stores (shops) and projects (council estates), slutty-looking girls and thuggish boys speaking a language she knew must be English but couldn't interpret for the life of her. (*They're only bored*, her friend Fiona insisted, *that savage youth non-sense is just media hysteria*), and probably Fiona was right, but then why were the papers and news filled with stories of youth crime, robberies and beatings and knifings, children torturing younger children, so much despair and rage? (*Because*, Ian told her, *in America, you lot are so used to it you've even given up reporting it unless it's done to some nice pretty blonde girl.*)

She was not blonde.

Other irrational hates included their wit—quicker and crueller than she was accustomed to—and the smell of chippies and kebab shops (*right*, Ian said, *'cause in America you've got no junk food, have you?*) and the different words for everything and the way people would tease her when she said the wrong (American) one, mocking her flat accent (or her insistence that she had no accent at all).

People who both bothered to notice her discomfort as well as care reassured her: *It's just an adjustment period. Culture shock. You'll get over it.*

After four months of togetherness, Ian had to leave. His work, which was some kind of consulting she never quite understood, took him all over the world, to exotic-sounding and sometimes hazardous places: Peshawar and Mumbai,

Mozambique, São Paolo and Dubai and Damascus. "What, he works for the MI6 then?" one of Fiona's friends asked with a laugh, and Penny laughed back and said, "No, something in computers," but the truth was she wasn't entirely certain and he wasn't very forthcoming. For all she knew maybe it *was* some kind of intelligence work. Back home in Portland he had seemed so forthright. She liked his strength, the way he made decisions for the both of them. She let herself be washed along in his wake. *Seduction* was such an old-fashioned word, but it had been just that, in more ways than one, from the moment he boldly asked her what time she finished at the Heathman hotel bar where she'd met him to his reckless proposal four weeks later, the day before he was meant to return home. In between he had consumed her, burning her up from the inside. They'd spent most of those four weeks in bed, when one or the other of them was not working. In the gaps between he was all she thought about: his hands and fingers, his mouth and his tongue, his cock, the warmth of him beside her as she drifted to sleep, where he followed her into dreams. She lost drink orders and made wrong change and served draft beer in dirty glasses. The manager gave her a talking-to. It didn't do any good.

People said things like *aren't you rushing into this* and *shouldn't you wait*. Had she any other choice? She could no more rush into something like breathing. The thought of him leaving without her made her physically ache, as though he were a phantom limb.

Now, he seemed secretive and distracted; maybe he had always been so.

Maybe, in the grip of the compulsion that was Ian, she had made a dreadful mistake.

She didn't actually allow herself to think *that*, not in so many words, but she came close, with the pregnancy scare, the days of frightened waiting, the knowledge that this would bind her more deeply to this man she hardly knew than even her own vulnerable flesh bound her, the overwhelming relief the shaky blue negative line on the plastic stick brought her.

You're so young, people had said, *you've your whole life ahead of you.* As if she was joining a nunnery, she laughed. As if! (Did they have nunneries nowadays? Did they call them that?) She was twenty-two years old. She had been on her own longer than most people her age and considerably longer than she liked. She had no close ties to speak of—an aunt in California, parents from whom she was long estranged. (A mundane story, like a thousand others: a broken home, absent father, disinterested mother, resentful stepfather.) She told most people she was marrying an Englishman and moving to London, even though he really came from the north, Birmingham, which sounded less romantic. (And on arriving there, she did indeed find that "romantic" was about the last word one might apply to the city.) It wasn't as though any of them would find out. Her friends at home, such as they were, had come to seem aimless and ragged and young, wearing themselves out on petty romantic and sexual dramas that were the prelude to a dismal settling at the end of it all. Yes, he was a bit older than her—thirty-eight, it wasn't so much. (It was a lot, and moreover, she felt he'd crammed two or three lifetimes into thirty-eight years. He was far more experienced and sophisticated than she. She was as flattered as she was baffled that she had captivated him.) She had left it all behind easily, without a backward glance or regret. At first the friends made overtures at staying in touch, popping into her chat window or sending Facebook invites, but by then they seemed unreal, and she preferred to let them disperse like so many molecules over the Atlantic.

And so, when the longing began to set in, she could not even say, really, what it was for.

Ian left without saying goodbye, in a rain-fogged October dawn. In fairness, she *was* feigning sleep, but it was mostly to see if he might make some loving farewell gesture while believing her to be unconscious. He did not.

She began in high spirits all the same. She had thought that she might try to find some kind of work to do, to keep herself occupied. Her papers were not yet in order to allow her legal employment, but Fiona and others she spoke to had friends and relatives who might get her in someplace, under the table. Just for a bit of pocket money and something to do. She told herself there was nothing condescending in these offers, even if *pocket change* and *something to do* was the sort of thing you arranged for bored teenagers. She said something to that effect to Fiona, who laughed and said, "Well, darling, you're scarcely finished being a teenager yourself."

Fiona was their next-door neighbour. She was very glamorous; she took photographs for a living and drove a fast red car. All of Ian's friends were quite a bit older than Penny. Most were reasonably kind in an absent-minded way, as though she were a pet they might scratch behind the ears before forgetting about her. A few were nasty, condescending. Fiona was older, too, but she was also one of the few who treated Penny like an actual person.

But it wasn't as easy to get that under-the-table job as everyone made it sound. Between ever-tightening immigration laws and an economy in shambles, no one was taking any chances. Penny came to her senses one morning standing over the sink sobbing. She thought, I have to get hold of myself. She raised her head; a fringe of curtain covered the lower section of the window and she could see out the top, see bare tree branches, broken black threads against a grey pillow of sky.

Out loud (and she often spoke out loud, because she got lonely and missed the sound of voices, her own and others), she said, "I'll go for a walk."

She went for lots of walks. It felt productive, even though it wasn't; it got her out of the house and even when the wind chapped her face and hands she felt moderately warmer than she did huddled indoors. She walked so much that she'd begun to grow lean, where before she'd been (she had to admit) a little chunky in places. The waistbands of her pants and skirts were too loose; her wool coat swallowed her up now. If she walked long enough and hard enough she might disappear, and then Ian would be sorry he'd left her alone.

At the bottom of the street—not the end with the pub, the other end—lay a wood, a thick and silent wood she liked to walk in; you imagined an urban wood would be noisy and crowded and littered with debris, used condoms and empty cider bottles and smashed beer cans, but this one was not and so she sometimes felt as though no one else knew of its existence. Among the trees, the tight leaden ball that had begun coiling in her stomach some months ago uncoiled and disappeared. When she emerged she inevitably felt renewed, and if she never could have quite said where in the wood she walked or what she saw there, well, she attributed that to the meditative state that the peaceful surroundings helped her achieve.

So it was that on that October day, tramping through the forest, a glint of metal caught her eye. Anger seized her—the first sign she'd seen of someone littering here, but as she bent down to pick it up, pulling it from the leaves, she realised it wasn't someone's carelessly discarded garbage.

She held in her hand a piece of jewellery, flat and perfectly round—a pin or brooch—silver, elaborately filigreed, and studded with little red stones, although some had been lost from their setting. She turned the piece over and over in her hands. Someone would be missing this. She wondered for a moment if she should put it back so the owner could retrace her steps and find it, but that was silly. She would take it with her and put up signs, run an advertisement.

Penny slipped the brooch into her pocket and started back toward home. She had only gone a few paces when she spotted a figure ahead of her. Perhaps this was the person who'd lost the brooch. To her surprise, a second rush of anger propelled her forward—how dare someone violate the peace of *her* forest? As she marched toward the figure, her fury dissipated. The figure was a woman. Her dark hair sprang wild and unmanageable, matted around a filthy face. Penny could see that beneath spatters of mud the woman's dress had once been brightly coloured; now it was thread-bare and torn in places. A heavy-looking cloak draped her shoulders. And then the woman spoke.

She spoke slowly, and with deliberation, but the words were gibberish to Penny—a language she'd never heard. "Do you speak English?" Penny asked. The woman's face darkened. She spat on the ground between them and turned, racing deeper into the forest.

Even had the woman not seemed feral and mad, even had she been a smiling stereotype of good middle-class English cheer, the woods were spoiled now for Penny. They were no longer hers. She walked home, sullen, and met Fiona in the driveway, just getting out of her car. "Darling!" said Fiona. Penny had never actually known anyone in real life who called people darling, but Fiona said it to everyone and it sounded normal coming from her. "Where have you been? Why don't you come in and get warmed up?"

Inside, over tea, Penny showed her the brooch. "I found it while I was out walking."

"It looks like the work a friend of mine does. She's a jewellery-maker," Fiona remarked. "She does replicas of Anglo-Saxon stuff, Celtic designs. Her work's quite popular. Someone will be missing this." She handed the brooch back, went to the bookshelf, and pulled out an oversized book, which she passed to Penny. "She does this kind of work."

Penny turned the pages. "What is all this?" Old stuff: she knew that much. Pictures of what looked like old manuscript scrolls covered in ancient writing; pictures of jewellery like her brooch; pictures of hammered cups and belts and platters. Sometimes, around Ian and his friends, she felt woefully undereducated. The book's title, *Anglo-Saxon Art and Design*, didn't shed any light for her.

"It's our history, not yours," Fiona said kindly. "Post-Roman Britain. About the sixth to the eleventh century. See, there it is." She pointed to a brooch that looked almost exactly like the one Penny had found.

"But not a real one," Penny said. "A replica, like you said with your friend."

"Well, unless you've stumbled on the find of the century on the streets of suburban Birmingham," Fiona said with a laugh. "And one man already did that, or practically that. Have you been to the museum? You can see the Staffordshire Hoard there; loads of pieces like those ones in the book."

Penny said, "I don't really like museums." She paged through the book a little more, until she came across a poem. A photograph of the manuscript itself was featured on one page and the facing page carried its translation, titled "The Wife's Lament". She read the beginning aloud to Fiona. "I tell this very melancholy tale about my fate. I may say what misery I endured after I grew up, whether new or old, never more than now. Always I knew misery, my journey of exile." Penny looked up. "Were they all this gloomy? Your ancestors, I mean?"

Fiona laughed again. "My ancestors were French."

Penny read on silently. "Even in regular English I can't understand it," she said. "It's a poem about this woman's husband, I think but I'm not sure. So, her lord leaves, and his kinsmen are evil to her. And then there's a lord, but you can't tell whether it's him or some new lord. He's 'ill-fortuned, sad-hearted, heart-concealing, murder-plotting.' And he commands that she 'be seized'. Listen to where they put her. 'Old is this earth-dwelling, I am consumed with longing. The dales are dark, the hills high, bitter enclosures overgrown with briars, a dwelling-place without joy.' "

"Good lord," Fiona said, "that doesn't sound very nice."

"What a horrible story," Penny said. The words worked on her in a way she couldn't describe. She had never liked poetry, never been one for reading much at all, for that matter, but these words conjured a series of vivid images, like she was watching it on film. A black and white film, in her imagination: the wife, standing by a twisted tree cracked by lightning, betrayed and exiled, cold wind whipping her cloak about her. And then her husband, a once-loved face turned cruel and mocking, forcing her into her grave.

She only then noticed Fiona looking at her funny. "You all right, love?"

"Can I borrow this book?"

Penny couldn't say why she didn't tell Fiona about the strange woman, and after drinking only half her tea excused herself; she found that she wanted to be alone, and to look at the book in privacy. The woman in the woods had spooked her, and everything around her felt shaky and unsure, as though she might at any moment pass her hand through a wall or begin sinking into the earth. Back in Ian's kitchen (why did she suddenly think of it that way? It was *their* kitchen, wasn't it?), she made her own cup of tea and wrapped her hands round it for warmth. The next thing she knew she was waking up in the big wingback chair in the sitting room; fortunately, she must have finished the tea before falling asleep—the cup was turned over on the carpet but nothing had spilled from it—but it had gone dark outside and she had no sense of the time. As she pulled herself up from the chair, she careened like a drunk. "Stop it," she said, holding onto the sound of her own voice again, and she closed her eyes and rested her hands on the back of the chair until the world got more solid around her. She peered at the clock over the mantel but her vision was too sleep-blurred to make out the numbers. "I've got a fever," she said, and then it all made sense. She was coming down with something. She should get to bed.

Fiona was standing over her, calling her darling again and helping her to sit up and giving her sips of water from a cup, and she had only a little time to wonder how Fiona had gotten into the locked house when Fiona announced firmly that they were off to the doctor and Penny wasn't to argue the point. Penny was, in fact, too weak to argue the point. Fiona helped her dress in a pair of sweatpants and a soft T-shirt and guided her out to the red sports car. The doctor took her temperature and looked at her throat and pronounced her to be suffering from strep throat and, perhaps, exhaustion (but what do I have to be exhausted about? Penny wondered. I never do anything or go any-where), gave her a shot of something to start her off, and sent her home with a bottle of antibiotic capsules. "You seemed so strange when I saw you yesterday," Fiona con-fided on the drive home, "and when I stopped over this morning and knocked on your door and you didn't answer, I got really worried." Penny remembered then to ask. "How did you get in?"

"I've got a key," Fiona said. "You know, Ian's gone so much, I used to check in on things now and again before the two of you . . . " She was rummaging in her purse and pulled out a cigarette, and didn't finish the sentence.

At that moment Penny knew. "You used to sleep with him, didn't you?" A wave of humiliation crashed over her, threatened to drown her. Maybe they were still sleeping together. Maybe they got together and laughed at her, at her youth and naiveté. *Everybody does it, darling. Don't be such a child*, Fiona might say.

Fiona lit the cigarette and smoked it fiercely. "It wasn't anything." Somehow that made it worse. How could it not be anything when it meant so much to Penny? Had the exquisite connection she'd imagined so unique when they first met been something very ordinary for Ian? "We're good friends and have been for years, but Ian adores you. Really he does—and it meant nothing, it was just something to do." Penny slumped miserably in her seat. When she closed her eyes she saw lights dancing against the back of her eyelids. She felt like shouting or crying, but her throat was too raw to do either.

It seemed doubly mortifying that she had to depend on Fiona to help her back into the house, into the big bed that she shared with Ian (that Fiona may have shared before her), that she had little choice but to agree that Fiona would look in on her again, that she felt herself sinking helplessly into sleep while Fiona was still bustling around the room.

She slept and she dreamed of a dark, hidden valley, with hills high and black all around her. The wind swept howling down the stark hills to the valley floor. She huddled in a ring of briars; each time she approached the edge of the ring, and tried to pass through it, the thorny branches thickened and seemed to come alive, weaving themselves into ever more tangled contortions. She became aware of a figure on the hillside, almost as dark as the hills themselves, and thought first to call out to it and then to hide herself from it among the briars. But then it came to her—she knew the figure was Ian, and she shouted at him, and even in the dream her throat felt ragged and painful. The figure turned, even though she couldn't have made herself heard at that distance. It wore Ian's face, but contorted, reproduced, and then frozen into a terrible mask, the features she loved turned sinister and twisted. Immediately she knew it had been a mistake to draw his attention.

She awoke with a start, tears still damp on her face. She could see through the opposite window that the day was clear and sunny: a rarity. She swallowed experimentally; the pain in her throat had receded, and the delirium of the fever seemed to have subsided. Gingerly, she climbed out of bed and made her way to the bathroom, where she stood under a hot spray, and afterward she dressed in regular street clothes—crumbling the things she'd worn while sick into a heap in the corner. She made her way downstairs and wondered what it would cost to have the locks changed.

She couldn't shake the images her mind kept thrusting upon her—Fiona and Ian upstairs in the bed together; Fiona on top of him, her back arched in ecstasy; Fiona kneeling in front of Ian, her face buried in his crotch. She felt betrayed, even though some part of her knew it was foolish. And what was Ian up to now anyway? He'd always been so vague about his work—or maybe it was her, just not understanding. But who was he with? She remembered how assured he'd been with her, how confident, as if he were used to seducing strange women he met in strange cities all the time. She'd been stupid to think she was special.

Her mobile jangled, and she jumped. She snatched it from the counter and read the text from Ian: *Hear you're sick babe. Better now I hope. Home early, dates to follow.*

Before she could think, she dialled his number back.

Ian's voice sounded very far away. "Penny? Is something wrong?"

"I just wanted to hear your voice."

"Listen," he said, as though she hadn't spoken, "like I said, I'm going to be able to come home early. We've wrapped up the project sooner than we thought."

Who are you? she thought. *What are you doing?* But she didn't say any of those things. Instead she said, "Okay."

In the background, wherever he was, she heard a woman's laughter. "You all right there? Not getting lonely? Fiona looking after you?"

"Yes."

"Great. Don't hesitate to call her if you need anything."

I hope I never see her again. "I won't." She took a deep breath. "Where are you?"

"What do you mean? I'm still in Johannesburg. You know that."

"No, I mean right now, where are you? I hear voices."

He sighed. "I'm at dinner with some people from the team, Penny. Would you like me to pass my mobile round to confirm that?"

She felt stung. He'd never talked to her like that before, never implied that she was jealous or suspicious. Fiona had definitely said something to him.

"I was just wondering," she said. "I miss you."

"I'll be home soon," he said, and she couldn't help noticing he didn't miss her back. "Day after tomorrow, looks like. Now I've got to run."

"I love you," she said to dead air.

She threw the phone down hard on the sofa and stalked into the kitchen, where she swallowed an antibiotic dry and then regretted it because it hurt her throat. Only then did she think to wonder what had become of the brooch.

What had she done with it before falling asleep in the chair? Surely Fiona wouldn't have taken it. She retraced her steps back into the sitting room and it was there, on the floor, probably where it had fallen from her hand. It was a pretty thing, even with the missing stones, and she could always get those replaced. There didn't seem to be much use in looking for the owner, really, and no way to ensure she'd get it to the right person anyway, and it all suddenly seemed too tiresome to think about.

The doctor had told her to take it easy, but a walk couldn't hurt. She was upset over the phone call; she needed to clear her head.

She wished there were some way to get down to the wood without passing Fiona's house. She kept her head down and walked more quickly than usual. But the woods held no solace for her today. She couldn't help noticing they were eerily quiet, and wondered if they'd always been that way— no rustling of small animals, no bird sounds. The absence of any signs of humans began to seem a more complete absence of life altogether. The trees looked diseased, their trunks mottled and unwholesome-looking, some of them twisted down toward the ground, broken-backed. Maybe everything was simply turning ugly in that way things did when it all began to go wrong. Penny turned back, headed in the direction of the house—it no longer seemed like "home".

The woman truly seemed to come out of nowhere this time, springing up from a crouch behind a withering oak tree, shouting something at her. She was close enough for Penny to smell her breath, which stank, and notice the ring of rotten teeth in her mouth. She snatched at Penny's chest, and only then did Penny realise she'd pinned the brooch there before leaving the house.

Penny stumbled backward, startled. The woman seized her by the shoulders. Her fingers, filthy, nails torn, scrabbled at the brooch. Penny gasped for breath and shoved. She turned and ran, one hand clutching the brooch, her feet slipping on dead leaves. She sobbed as she ran, all the way up the street, like a madwoman. Her hands shook as she jammed her key in the lock, and she slammed the door shut behind her and stood shuddering against it.

When she undressed for another shower, which she hoped would somehow purge the memory of the woman's face thrust into hers, she was unsurprised to see big purple bruises staining her shoulder blades, like the woman's finger-marks tattooed on her body. The shower was only lukewarm this time and then ran cold. She was shivering when she stepped out. Her body ached; she had overexerted herself while still ill, and it was only her imagination running away with her that in her recollection, the woman's face had been her own—ravaged by unimaginable suffering, perhaps disease, but her own features all the same.

She pulled the duvet off the bed and dragged it downstairs, where she lay on the sofa and felt miserable. She was going to have to get hold of herself before Ian came home. Some of his friends treated her like a child, but now she was really acting like one.

She reached for the book Fiona had loaned her and flipped through its pages again. She could almost imagine that the woman's dress was not unlike those worn by the women sketched in the book. She found the poem again, and read, "Friends are in the earth, lovers in life, occupying beds. Then I at dawn walk alone, under the oak-tree around this earth-grave."

She never knew when she crossed into a dream; while she lay on the sofa, trees sprouted and misshaped themselves all around her, some bearing sickly-coloured flowers that blossomed noxiously. Hands gripped her, forcing her beneath the tree and trapping her there, and then she began to dig, first frantically, like a dog, then wearily but unceasing. She felt herself aging as she burrowed into the earth. One of the hands clenched her and would not let go, and she finally succeeded in twisting her body round to see who held her. Ian's face grinned and grinned; this was not the sinister look he'd borne in her earlier dream, but it was all the worse for his uninhibited glee at her suffering.

She woke with a start and for a moment felt the earth-grave still beneath her, rocks and branches under her back, insects squirming and churning by her ears. She lay for a long time before she trusted herself to get up. She picked up her phone to check the time; an entire day had passed, and it was morning again. At this rate, missing the antibiotics, running about the streets, she was never going to get well.

Penny rose wearily this time. She felt ancient. She didn't bother with another shower, or even combing her hair or brushing her teeth. She let herself out the front door and went over to Fiona's. She'd barely touched the knocker when Fiona opened it.

"Darling," she said. "I saw you coming up the front path. You look awful. You haven't been following doctor's orders, have you?"

Penny burst into tears. Fiona hustled her inside, set her down in a cosy chair in the front room next to a fire. "I'm such an idiot," Penny confessed between sobs. "I've been acting like such a baby about you and Ian, like you two deliberately did something to hurt me. And Ian called and I acted—stupid, all suspicious of him, and there's a woman in the woods down at the end of the road who's freaking me out."

Fiona was staring at her. "What woods do you mean?"

"At the bottom of the street." Penny pointed.

Fiona was silent for several moments, and they sat staring at one another. Finally Fiona said softly, "Penny, there are no woods around here. At the bottom of the street is an office park. Look, I'll show you," and she made to help her up gently, but Penny pulled away. This was really too much. Why would Fiona do this to her—*were* they conspiring? "Don't touch me," Penny snapped as she got to her feet. "Leave me alone." Back at home, she closed the curtains and stuck a chair under the knob of both the front and back door for good measure. She still couldn't think why Fiona would say such a thing; it was absurd. The woods were there; they had always been there, same as the house, and the road outside, and Fiona, and Ian, same as anything. And yet when Penny tried to think back, to picture the look of the woods at the bottom of the street from the sidewalk in front of the house, she could not; neither could she remember how she'd found her way to them, or when she first began walking there.

She was afraid to go outside and have a look.

Instead, she went online, and began reading about the history of the area. There had been a wood there, long ago, she read—indeed, over a thousand years ago it seemed much of Birmingham itself had once been part of the great Forest of Arden, unspoiled even by Roman roads. Penny closed the browser and shut off the computer. She felt worse, not better, for her enquiries.

The day passed in a fever of anxiety. A dozen times she went to the door to open it; as many times she stopped, hand on the doorknob, and stepped away. She kept the curtains pulled but when she flicked them back a couple of times the sky outside was dark as if the day had never dawned, and by afternoon heavy showers had rolled in. The house was cold and cheerless.

She could not stop thinking about what Ian might be doing, what he must be doing; he was waking up with a girl that worked at the restaurant where he'd had the meal he called her from, with a co-worker, with Fiona. He was next door with Fiona right now, and they were laughing at her. He'd never left town at all. She had never before known that the word *heartache* meant an actual pain in the chest, heavy and suffocating.

She fell asleep wrapped in a blanket in the big wingback chair, and woke to the sound of someone pounding on the door and swearing. Something crashed on the floor. Penny leapt to her feet, still sleep-fogged, and then Ian stalked in.

"What the hell is going on?"

She stood blinking at him for several moments before she remembered. "Oh," she said. "The chair. I didn't want Fiona to come over."

"Fiona," he said. He didn't greet her; he didn't say hello, or kiss her, or tell her that he'd missed her. He stared at her, a stern stranger. In his absence, she had almost forgotten what the real Ian was like: how tall he was, how neat and impeccable in his dress, how he seemed to command any space he was in. "She's worried about you. She told me about the wood at the bottom of the street. Penny, I think you need to see a doctor. Not about your cold, or whatever it is." He said it impatiently, like she was faking it. "Fiona says there's something wrong with you."

Of course Fiona would say that, wouldn't she? With Penny out of the way, she could have Ian back.

"Fiona misunderstood me," Penny said.

Did some aroma of another woman's perfume waft around him? The clichéd lipstick on his collar? What had he been doing those weeks away in Johannesburg? Was he there at all?—had he even gone to South Africa? She glanced at his suitcase; the baggage claim tag, if there had been one, was already removed.

"I had her make an appointment for you," he said. "You go in tomorrow." He went past her, into the kitchen. She could hear the sounds of ice clinking against a glass. In the space of a moment, it came to her that she was utterly alone in the world. She and Ian had no past, no history over which to build the bridge that would take them to the other side of this moment. And his own past was a mystery to her. Had he even been married before? She had not thought to ask, and he was not forthcoming. He had said he had no family, and as she didn't either, she'd thought nothing about it at the time. It had never occurred to her to ask him about anything he had not volunteered.

Penny pushed off the duvet and got to her feet. She had a moment of seeing herself from the outside, how she must appear: un-showered, sickly, still in her pyjamas. She looked crazy. She felt crazy. She called after him, "I don't need to go to the doctor. I already went."

He strode back in, carrying his drink. "A different kind of doctor," he said.

She said, "What kind of work do you do? Where do you go? It isn't computers, is it?"

He stared at her. "Penny," he said wearily, "stop it. This has nothing to do with me. This is in your head. Fiona says you're imagining all sorts of things." For a moment his features slipped and he became the sinister Ian of her dream, and then the mask dropped again. She knew what the doctor would say—that she was crazy, that she needed medication, maybe. Maybe they would put her away some-place against her will.

More kindly, then, Ian said, "You should try to sleep. I've got some pills to help you, if you want them."

"I won't need that," she said stiffly, belatedly hoping to regain some measure of dignity. She went upstairs without an-other word, dressed in her nightgown, and crawled into bed.

She was startled awake by him. It might have been min-utes or hours later. A storm appeared to have rolled in during the night, and she could hear the wind and rain lashing at the window, rattling the glass. Ian was tearing at her nightgown, forcing himself inside her. She was unready, and she gasped in pain and shock, then again as waves of pleasure seized her, sobbing at what felt like betrayal by both Ian and her own body. She couldn't see Ian's face, masked as it was by the darkness. When he had finished he rolled off her. She was too frightened to speak to him; she was not even certain he had ever been awake.

When he had not moved again for some time, she crept from the bed to the window. Outside in the back garden, the woman was waiting.

Penny scrambled about the bedroom in the dark in search of the brooch. Perhaps returning it to the woman would put a stop to things. Perhaps then she could start to piece herself together again. Ian rolled over, snoring. She found the brooch in the top drawer of her dresser. She slipped down the stairs and out the back door.

The wind tore at her hair and the rain soaked her in seconds. The woman was no longer in the back garden, but Penny knew where she could find her. Fiona and everyone else might say no wood lay at the bottom of the street, but everyone was wrong. Didn't that happen sometimes, that one person knew the truth, and everyone around them was wrong? She wished she had grabbed a coat as she raced up the street, but she had no time to turn back now. Penny plunged into the forest.

The rain lessened once she found herself under the canopy of trees, and then stopped. If the forest had seemed sickly and diseased earlier, now it was all but dead. Its misshapen trees had gone white and ghostly, thin fingers of leafless branches pale against the storm-wracked sky. The earth reeked of decay. Thick ropy briar fences replaced the vegetation that had once grown there. Only her panting breath stirred the silence. The brooch hurt her hand; she was gripping it too tightly, cutting into her own flesh, but she could not let it go.

She had a sense of the woman somewhere just ahead of her, but she feared that if she called out to her it would only frighten her. She was brought up short when she came to the tree split by lightning, the tree she'd seen in her imagination. She cast about for the woman, but she was nowhere to be seen. Perhaps she could bury the brooch.

Penny dropped to her knees and clawed at handfuls of soil. She could hear her own breath, ragged and wheezing. As she scrabbled at the ground she noticed her hands—hands she did not recognise as her own, filthy, with fingers ending in shattered, dirt-crusted nails. She lifted them before her face, touched her hair, and found it thick and matted. The soft fabric of her nightgown had turned heavy and coarse. She thought she had put the brooch down on the leaves beside her, but now it clutched the heavy cloak too tightly about her neck, choking her.

A figure she'd mistaken for the woman emerged from the trees beyond, and then another. For one moment she fancied them rescuers, but then some of them gripped her and held her, while others dug at the base of the tree.

She fought them. She kicked at them, she spat and she scratched and she wailed and she wept, but they were too strong and too many for her. *The man commanded me to dwell in a grove of trees under an oak tree in this earth's grave.* She would not leave this place. *I at dawn walk alone under the oak-tree around this earth-grave.* She would not leave this wood, the wood they'd told her could not exist. The world of office parks, of chippers and pubs, was gone; or rather, it had yet to be. It might never be.

She could not see their faces. Surely one of them was Ian, indifferent and cruel, or someone like him. Her strength was ebbing. The limbs of the dead whitened trees joined the human hands that forced her into the ground, as the earth itself embraced her. She heard herself as if from someplace distant, keening like a lost girl, forgotten and unloved, and the mist lowered and the rain began to fall again as the forest closed in on the lamenting wife and was no more.

For Christine Rose

This Time of Day, This Time of Year

Josie came back. At first, that was all that mattered. Not Basra or Baghdad, not Falluja, not Karbala or Samarra or any of the other cities and towns and villages whose names and existences had been unknown to them until they became places where Josie might be lost to them forever. Those didn't matter, nor did—it had to be said—Josie herself, somehow changed, diminished. No, it only mattered that Josie came back, and her parents and brothers and sisters and aunts and uncles and cousins and the whole community rejoiced. That first Sunday in church the new preacher announced it from the pulpit, beaming like they were welcoming some kind of angel of God into their midst. Josie was home again, safe back in Georgia in the womb of family, protected from harm.

Of course, Ellen was happy that Josie was home. Of course she was. Ellen was the youngest of five kids and apt to get left out of things, only because people still thought of her as a baby, and she wasn't, she was nearly thirteen (well, next year), and that was a long way from babyhood. But she and Josie had always been extra close. Not Ellen with Beth, the sister nearest her own age, and not Josie with Beth, who'd been Josie's sister first, and thus longer. No, it was always Josie and Ellen, never mind the eight years between them. They even looked alike: pale and brown-haired and skinny in a family of blondes. Beth had been barely a year old when Ellen was born, and so a lot of Ellen's care fell to Josie, to ease the burden on their mother. As Josie got older she never seemed to mind her baby sister tagging along, like to the mall with friends. When she went to the fair with her boyfriend, she brought Ellen along. Everybody was so used to seeing the two of them together that no one thought about it much.

So Ellen was overjoyed when she heard they were sending Josie home. Like everyone else, she didn't care about the details—and there seemed to be a lot of details. All she thought was of having Josie back where they could touch her and keep her safe. Ellen had gone around sick to the stomach that whole year waiting for bad news. Whenever she heard of a soldier or a journalist kidnapped in Iraq or Afghanistan or Pakistan, she pictured Josie tied up, her eyes frightened above a filthy cloth stuffed in her mouth. Her brother Byron, who was fifteen, heard you could see *videos* of people getting decapitated on the internet; he showed her one and never before in her life had she wanted to unthink something the way she did that. Byron felt bad afterwards. He said the videos were probably faked by some sicko. In some ways that was worse: now she not only knew what happened to some people Over There, but that some people Right Here might look on it as entertainment.

But Josie was here now, so Ellen didn't have to imagine her flesh rotting, bones bleaching in a desert somewhere. At first there was just that: gladness and relief. Then they pretended for a while, when they started noticing things were not right with Josie—and they started noticing pretty fast—but they didn't talk about it. They pretended everything was okay, because that's what families do.

So Ellen never knew if she'd been the first to start noticing or someone else was. Cole was a senior in high school that year and started staying late at football practice every night. Soon Beth had play rehearsals that stretched longer than they ought and a steady stream of overnights at other girls' houses. Their mother used to not let them stay with friends on a school night, but after Josie came back, a lot of things fell by the wayside, and all their mother ever said about it was that Beth was about old enough that she soon wouldn't want to do that anymore—soon she'd rather be out with boys—so she might as well enjoy herself.

They all found ways of being a little more absent than usual.

Ellen was glad that Josie was back, but all the same, when Josie said she wanted to go to Uncle Hugh's summerhouse for a spell, Ellen's first thought wasn't how bad she wanted to go with her. Josie was not right at all: she was sleepwalking, for one thing, stalking into the kitchen and sitting down across from you like some kind of zombie, and when she wasn't doing that she was crying out from nightmares. She brooded. She snapped at everyone. She was listless. She showed little interest in the things she used to love: running, reality TV, or tinkering with her car, the 1970 Ford Mustang she'd worked so hard saving up for all through high school. She ignored calls and visits from old friends. The only thing that made living with her bearable at all was the overcrowded house—with the seven of them—which had always seemed like a pain until now. Now the numbers were a buffer against Josie's strangeness. At Uncle Hugh's summerhouse it would just be Ellen and Josie—for by then Josie had asked Ellen to go along—and there would be no escaping her.

"Oh, Josie, I don't know," their mother said. "Nobody's even been out there in years. I'm sure it's filthy. Maybe it's not even secure—maybe it's broken into or something."

"I'm not afraid of vandals," Josie said significantly, letting them know she'd faced down scarier things than a dirty cabin with a broken lock.

"Anyway, it looked okay from the outside." Josie had already gone out there once or twice, leaving at dawn before anyone got up and returning at dusk.

"You just spent the day out there swimming?" Ellen had asked, and Josie shrugged and said sure, in that diffident way she said so many things these days.

Ellen waited for her reprieve, but none came. "You go with your sister," their mother said, "she needs you." Ellen appealed to their father, who worked long hours at his auto shop and wasn't around much. He never talked a whole lot. He didn't then, either. "She's your sister, Ellie. You do the right thing," was all he said. Their mother went to Ellen's principal to talk about her missing school for a few days. Normally Mrs. Rice was inflexible on such matters, but this called her patriotic duty into question; she arranged for Ellen's teachers to send some work home for Ellen to complete. And that was that.

So to the summer place they went, albeit in autumn. "The summer place" was a far grander name than it deserved. It was really just a one-room cabin Uncle Hugh had built for fishing trips and the like or—truth was, nobody really knew why he'd done it. He'd bought a patch of land out at Sorrow Lake and built the cabin and went out there to "get away from it all" as he said. Though as a bachelor, he couldn't really be said to have things in his life that needed getting away from, at least not things that necessitated a whole separate residence. It was true he'd come back from Desert Storm with a whole set of ailments the VA doctors said were all in his head; when he drank, he was prone to accuse the government of using him as a human guinea pig, but Ellen had only heard these stories second-hand, she'd been too young to remember any of it herself.

When Ellen's siblings and cousins started going out to the summerhouse, Uncle Hugh had torn down the outhouse and put in plumbing, and added a couple of bunk beds to the Spartan living space. That was the extent of his upgrades. Apparently, overnight invitations to the summerhouse had been quite a treat for the older kids—midnight swims and junk food feasts and all-nighters with minimal supervision—but then Uncle Hugh had tragically drowned in the lake when Ellen was five. His body had not been recovered—the lake was enormous, with miles of shore-line—and Ellen's mother had felt it an affront to sell off the place when there was the slightest chance Uncle Hugh might, as she put it, "come walking back through there again someday," and she'd nod at the screen door off the kitchen when she said it, but the years had passed and Uncle Hugh had not done so, and she said it less and less.

Family lore had it that Ellen was heartbroken at Uncle Hugh's passing, but if so, this had long since vanished from her memory. Her older siblings and cousins could sit around indulging for hours in remember-whens, which only served to emphasise the distance between them—not only the youngest in her immediate family, but the youngest of the cousins. She was practically an afterthought.

As it turned out, the lock on the summerhouse was se-cure. No squatters or vandals had defiled the premises. But it was filthy: cob- and spider-webby, furry with dust and skittering with roaches. The trickle of water from the sink was brown, so they ran it until it was clear. Josie had never been one for cleaning up, but she directed the operation. They drove back into town and got mops, brooms, dust-cloths, fresh sheets (the ones in the summerhouse were yellowed and spattered with mildew), dish detergent, bug spray, soaps, and rubber gloves. By evening the cabin was passable; too primitive to ever feel spic-and-span, but at least you didn't feel like your lungs would collapse from breath-ing in there, or that you'd get a disease eating off the plates.

They had baked beans and frankfurters, heated on Uncle Hugh's little hotplate, which still worked. They ate sitting right next to each other on the concrete stoop at the front door, because even though it was October the nights were still warm. They were sweaty, too, from cleaning; they both wanted showers but the rusty showerhead didn't work. Josie said they'd go back to town and pick up one of those solar showers, but in the meantime they could take a dip in the river.

"Shouldn't we wait an hour after eating?" Ellen asked, but Josie said that was an old wives' tale, so they put on their bathing suits and flip flops and got their towels. They followed a trail carpeted with pine needles through the woods to the lot where people left their cars to walk down to the river. There was an artificial beach with sand leading down to the water. The opposite shore was thick with pine trees. "Swim At Your Own Risk. No Lifeguard on Duty", a sign advised, because Sorrow Lake had a bad reputation for swimming and boating accidents. In fact it was called by a different name on the maps, an official name that no one could ever remember. It had been called Sorrow Lake after seven engineers drowned there during its construction, or so the story went. Every year a few people were lost here, just like Uncle Hugh, and the local paper would run stern editorials about the dangers of combining alcohol with boating and swimming, and no one ever seemed to take heed.

This time of day, and this time of year, nobody else was around. The season was dying. The sun, fat and orange, had begun to sink into the water, spraying reds and purples across the horizon. Josie went in first, running into the water and dipping below the surface. Seeing her like that, from behind, Ellen realised how thin her sister was. No meat on her bones at all, just skin over stringy muscles and fragile bone. She thought about it: Josie had eaten okay, she guessed—the beans and frankfurters—but she couldn't remember her finishing a meal since her return, and she often stayed in her room at dinner, saying she'd get something later. Later, Ellen now realised, generally never came.

She followed her sister in gingerly. The water had cooled along with the season. It was good to feel the grime and sweat washing away, and she ducked under to rinse her hair, but the water was so cold it gave her a headache, and she quickly retreated to the shore, huddling under a towel while Josie gambolled in the water. That was the word that came to Ellen—gambolling—she'd learned it the week before in English class, and it perfectly described her sister's movements. She seemed carefree for the first time since before she left for Iraq.

That night in the bottom bunk Ellen couldn't sleep, but Josie, dreamless and peaceful, snored soundly for nine hours. Lying awake, Ellen wondered what they'd do with themselves next. They couldn't just swim all day. She wished she hadn't come with Josie; she almost wished Josie had never come home, the way she was now.

Ellen fell asleep at last just before dawn, and when she woke up the cabin was empty. She dressed and walked down to the river. The surface looked calm until Josie broke from it. With her hair plastered around her head she reminded Ellen of a seal or a sea lion. Ellen waved but Josie didn't seem to notice, and dived back under again. She was down so long that Ellen started to worry; then she bobbed back into view, lifted her head, and finally waved back, shouting something that Ellen couldn't hear.

Josie swam to shore.

"Let's go back into town," she said. "I want to get that solar shower and we'll need goggles or masks or something like that. Maybe flippers." She didn't say why they needed all those things.

They made their second trip to Wal-Mart; in the parking lot they saw one of Josie's best friends from high school and Josie hid behind an SUV and made Ellen hide too. "I'm just not ready to talk to people yet," she mumbled. They got everything Josie wanted at the store and drove back to the cabin in silence. Ellen's stomach was growling—they'd eaten nothing since the beans and frankfurters—but Josie wanted to go back into the water immediately. Ellen stayed back at the cabin, dozing on the bottom bunk after her sleepless night. Near evening she woke up and made herself a pimento cheese sandwich—Uncle Hugh's little fridge still worked—and sat out in front of the cabin working on some math problems.

Josie came back after sunset. It didn't seem safe, swimming alone in the dark, but Ellen didn't know what she could do about it. She wished their cell phone worked but she hadn't been able to get a signal, and what if Josie became unruly or aggressive or had some kind of breakdown? But that was crazy; Josie was calmer and happier, and to Ellen's relief, she ate, too. Pimento cheese, and the last of the baked beans. She said they'd put up the shower in the morning.

Ellen hadn't found a way to raise the subject of leaving, but the solar shower remark didn't bode well for imminent departure. That night Josie was restless. She started shouting, and Ellen called her name over and over to wake her. Suddenly Josie was hanging her top half off the mattress above, hair streaming down in the moonlight. It ought to have been funny but it looked awful, like she'd turned into some sort of monster. The light from the moon showed streaks of tears on her face.

Josie said, "Ellen, what's Cole doing after high school?" Sometimes Josie asked pointed questions like that, about what somebody was up to, and Ellen would realise how out-of-it she really was. Everyone knew Cole had already joined the Marines and was heading off to basic as soon as the school year ended.

Josie flopped back onto the top bunk after Ellen said it, and Ellen felt bad that she was glad she didn't have to look at Josie's face anymore. "I can't believe somebody else in this family is doing something that stupid," Josie said.

Ellen didn't know what to say. There wasn't anything they could do about Cole—she was pretty sure you couldn't back out once you'd signed up. Not unless, like with Josie, they had some reason to send you home. And she didn't know why Josie was so surprised—lots of boys and girls from their town went into the military right after high school.

What Ellen said was,

"I thought the war was supposed to be ending. Josie, do you know we've been at war my whole life?" Josie didn't answer for a while, and when she did, her voice sounded different. "Not your whole life, hon, but probably for as long as you can remember." The dark made Ellen braver. "So what did you do over there?"

"A lot of the time it was pretty boring. But one time . . . "

Ellen waited for Josie to finish. She counted to a hundred, waited some more counted to a hundred again, and said, "What about the one time?"

"Never mind," Josie said. "Go to sleep."

"I'm not sleepy."

Josie leaned back down from the top bunk.

"What somebody needs to tell Cole is that they're lying to him. There's no glory waiting for him. After a while, everywhere I looked I saw y'alls faces on dead people—you or Beth or Mama or Byron. And there's other stuff, too, but I'm not gonna tell you about any of it, Ellie, just go to sleep."

But Ellen couldn't, and she knew Josie couldn't either. She heard Josie holding herself still, but restless, breathing the way people do when they're awake and trying to hide it, all through the night and past the dawn.

She didn't dare ask the other question, the real one: *So why did they send you home early?*

First thing next morning Josie said, "Let's put up the solar shower." They found a tree with a suitable limb and enough sunshine to hang the bag. Josie said it would heat up in a few hours, but in the meantime she was going for a swim. Ellen stayed behind and ate cornflakes, which tasted dusty, like the cabin, even though they'd just bought them. Afterwards she did some social studies homework (*Read chapter four and answer these questions about European explorers in the Americas*) and when Josie still wasn't back, she decided to head down to the river.

Today they weren't alone, and this somehow surprised her; she'd started to imagine they had their own private beach. This other person wasn't swimming, though. A small woman with an easel and a bright red unruly brush of hair was painting, squinting at the canvas, then at the river, then at the canvas again. Coming closer, Ellen saw the woman wasn't painting a riverside scene at all. Taking shape on the canvas was a street scene, though not in any present-day town. People rode in horse-drawn buggies, and men wore hats, while women were in long dresses.

The painter turned as Ellen approached. She had a round, friendly face. "Looks like we've got the place to ourselves," she said Ellen resented her presumption of belonging to any group that included herself and Josie.

"Is that your mom out there?" the woman asked, undaunted, and Ellen shook her head. "My sister." Her curiosity overcame her irritation then, and she asked, "Why are you looking at the river but painting that?"

"Oh, that." The woman looked at the canvas distractedly. "That's Hekate. They flooded the town when they built the dam and created the lake back in the fifties, but it was dead decades before that."

Ellen moved closer. "A town," she said, pointing at the lake. "Here?"

"Mmm hmm. They named the lake for it, you know. Lake Hekate . . . "

Ellen said, "Nobody calls it that."

The woman nodded towards a canvas bag on its side next to her. "Look in those books."

Ellen pulled out a battered hardcover that smelled like mildew. The faded gilt lettering on the side said "Towns of Old Georgia". The book featured a lot of pictures which were noted to be "artists" renderings. She flipped through it until she came to the chapter on Hekate.

> The town of Hekate was founded in 1790 by Diony-
> sius Campbell along the Savannah and Broad Rivers,
> and named for his mother's birthplace in Greece. For
> more than fifty years Hekate was a thriving town,
> the largest in the region. It boasted a bank, a hotel,
> a church, a school, a grog shop, and a number of
> private homes . . .

Ellen said, "So what happened to it?"

"It just died out. Flip ahead a few pages."

Ellen flipped ahead and read,

"Although the town had begun to show signs of de-population and decline by the 1840s, an epidemic—now thought to have been Yellow Fever—wiped out many inhabitants in the early 1850s. The Civil War, however, proved its death knell; the men-folk of the town marched off to battle, and those who returned were said to have been 'ravaged' by starvation and suffering. Within a year of the war's end, the town was all but abandoned."

The woman said, "When the water level's low, like the last couple of years, you can see some of the foundations. All that rain this spring brought the level back up again. Oh, and that book gets some things wrong. Hekate's not the name of a town in Greece, or anywhere else that I know of. Hekate was a Greek goddess."

Ellen couldn't stop staring at the surface of the lake, imagining the roads that lay beneath, the school maybe, stores, and homes—places people had loved, they felt safe, places where they had hoped to live out their lives. She said, "It seems so sad, though."

The woman stopped painting and looked at Ellen full in the face. "It does, doesn't it?" she said. "All that industry, just gone to nothing. It's a microcosm of the end of humanity."

Ellen didn't understand the last thing she said, and her face felt hot under the woman's scrutiny, though it was a cool morning. She mumbled something and the woman turned to look out at Josie. "I think your sister's part mermaid."

They watched as Josie turned to shore. She waded out and walked over towards them, shooting wary glances at the stranger.

"Hey Josie, did you know there's a whole *city* under that lake?"

"Sure. Everybody knows that."

"I didn't."

"It's not really a city," said the red-haired woman. "It's a town. And not really a town, not anymore. Just some old foundations. Nothing else left of it."

Josie fixed her with a look. "What do *you* know about it?"

Ellen thought the woman would get flustered, but she gazed calmly back at Josie. "I teach history at the university," she said "This regional stuff is my specialty."

Josie said, "Ellen, it's lunchtime. Let's go."

This was the first time Josie had expressed any interest in mealtimes, or even awareness of them. Back at the cabin Ellen made herself another pimento cheese sandwich. She wasn't really hungry, but she hoped Josie would follow her example. Josie watched her slathering the bread and demanded, "Who was that woman? How do you know her?"

Ellen felt angry with her sister for the first time since she'd come home. "Chill," she snapped. "She was just some stupid woman painting by the lake. What's wrong with you anyway?"

Josie pushed past her and slammed the door hard on her way out of the cabin. Ellen sat on her bunk, moodily chewing the sandwich she hadn't wanted in the first place.

She threw the rest of it away and followed Josie outside. She'd thought Josie would be back at the lake, but Josie was pacing the scrubby patch of pine needles near the car. Ellen didn't know what to say, so she opened her mouth and words just spilled out.

"Is that why you wanted the mask and stuff?" she said. "Are you exploring at the city under there? Is there anything left? Is it cool?" She pictured it: fish darting in and out of vacant windows, doors swinging gently with the motion of the water, roads that led to nothing.

Josie stopped pacing. "Why don't you come with me?"

Ellen remembered how cold the water had been. She thought how much colder it would be deeper and farther out, but she couldn't shake the images in her head.

By the time they got down to the lake, the woman was gone. Ellen sat down and pulled on flippers, which were too large and felt awkward, and the mask. "Stay close to me," Josie said. "I'll show you where to go. Do exactly as I do."

"Is it safe?" Ellen said, suddenly worried, and Josie snapped, "Of course it isn't."

They waded out till the water reached Ellen's chest, and then they swam. The lake was just as cold as she'd remembered. She was a good swimmer, though, and kept up with her sister, heading towards the middle of the lake. Taking a deep breath, they dived beneath the surface.

Down they went, deeper and deeper, and she could feel the pressure growing in her ears. Where was Josie going? How deep was the lake? Would her eardrums burst? Could they die? But Josie'd done this many times, and she seemed fine. Well, as fine as Josie ever was these days.

Further down, and Ellen began to feel disoriented. She could no longer see the surface. It seemed like long, long minutes had passed, but that couldn't be possible. She was glad for the mask, and kept her gaze on Josie just ahead. Around her everything was black.

And then the drowned village swam into view; Hekate, flooded with light.

The historian-woman on the shore had been wrong. Much more than foundations remained; Hekate looked more like Ellen had imagined: whole streets were laid out, lined with houses and shops. Their approach was a dizzying experience. She'd never been on a plane before, and she wondered if it felt anything like this. Descending into a town from above made her feel like some sort of god.

Later, Ellen tried to remember Hekate, but the images came as if from a dream, fragmented and impossible. She could read the names on some of the buildings: Cassidy's Hotel, Scarborough's Dry Goods, A & R Savings and Loan. She and Josie swam through windows and out of doorways amid fast-moving schools of reddish fish. Ellen shivered as their scaly bodies flicked against her flesh. Then she was losing track of Josie, and swimming faster, sure that the drowned city was still inhabited, that if only she could move more swiftly she could catch them. Soft vibrations buzzed in her ears like voices, just elusive enough to be her imagination.

At the end of the main street lay a crumbling church, the pews still intact but no roof. Its stained glass windows had survived, congealed with green slime. Surely the glass should have shattered under the pressure? But if that was so, surely she and Josie should be shattered as well? Later, when the town had come to dominate her dreams, Ellen thought she must have imagined the church, because the imagery she could make out in the stained glass somehow didn't seem suitable for church. In fact, the more Ellen saw, the more she wished she hadn't, and the harder it was to look away. They compelled her to look, even as she felt for the first time a heaviness in her chest, the pressure of the water above her increasing. The figure of a woman caught her eye, no modest Biblical figure but a woman with eyes so dark and terrible Ellen found herself lost in them, and overcome with the need to breathe. Just one breath.

Something took her arm—Josie, pointing straight up, and up they went in a whirling rush. Breaking into the bright air Ellen gasped and sobbed as oxygen returned to her lungs.

They swam back without a word, exhausted, and wrapped themselves in their towels.

At last Ellen asked, "How was that possible?"

"What?"

"Everything," Ellen said. "How we went so deep, and that we didn't need to breathe. And how the town was so . . . intact. Not like that woman said."

"Well, she didn't know what she was talking about."

"But what about the other stuff?"

Josie's laugh sounded forced. "You have a big imagination," she said. "The water level's not that high. You can see the town without going very deep as long as you have a mask, and we were only under a few minutes. You have good lungs!"

Ellen knew Josie was lying, though her memory of the place was already fraying, bleeding out imperceptibly to the dream periphery of her mind. She could still remember those sibilant voices, and the soft whisper of the water rippling through empty windows and abandoned doorways.

They could only have been under a few minutes at most, and had not even swum as far as the middle of the lake. Josie insisted. And of course nothing else was possible. Yet Ellen was sure the sun had changed position in the sky.

Josie slept soundly that night. Ellen did not. She tossed and turned, dreaming fitful underwater dreams of a forgotten world and its watery inhabitants. Morning broke grey and still, with a hint of cool weather ahead. Ellen knew when she opened her eyes that she was alone in the cabin again.

She pushed back the covers, dressed hurriedly and made her way down to the lake.

Josie's towel was there, but she herself was nowhere to be seen.

She'd surface soon. She couldn't stay underwater more than a few minutes. Ellen sat down on her sister's towel. She didn't have a watch, so she counted. She counted what seemed like four minutes, and it was fair to think maybe she'd counted too fast, and so she counted another four minutes, and then there was no guessing to be done, Josie had been under far too long.

Ellen's mind seemed to stop short at that, but her limbs took over; she felt she was watching herself from far away— the girl who scrambled to her feet, who ran up the path to the parking lot. She thought she'd seen a public phone there (please let it not be broken, let it work, let it work). It wasn't a pay phone but a direct emergency phone, for just such an occasion, for there was, as the sign cautioned, "No Lifeguard On Duty", and Sorrow Lake was aptly named. And she tore the phone from its cradle and said things she couldn't remember, and then her arms and legs decided they'd done their job, and she sank to the asphalt and waited for someone else to say what happened next.

Even though nothing would ever feel normal again, Ellen was relieved to find herself back in the room she shared with Beth, back in the gentle chaos of the crowded family. And since Josie had been gone the whole of last year anyway, she could almost pretend nothing had happened. Or she could be like her mother: Josie might come walking through that door any day, since they hadn't found her, so just because her towel was on the shore and her car parked by the cabin, it didn't mean she'd drowned, didn't mean she was lost to them forever.

Ellen's mother put the summerhouse up for sale, along with its little plot of land. A man bought it that winter. Then winter gave way to spring and school was out again and Cole went off to basic but not to Iraq like his sister; that war, they said, was ending. They sent Cole to Afghanistan.

Ellen spent a lot of time at the library that summer. She liked reading, and she didn't want to be around the house any more than she had to. Josie's vanishing (for she could only think of it like that) went deeper than any word like pain or loss or even death could explain. A great emptiness yawned at her back, an unspeakable extinction, and she might as well have led Josie straight there, sleeping peacefully while Josie went to her fate. Her inability to save her sister consumed every waking hour and even her dreams.

Partway through summer she summoned the courage to talk to a reference librarian, and ask for help researching the town of Hekate. The librarian was eager but bemused.

"It can't be for school," she said, "so just research on your own?" and Ellen nodded. The librarian probably talked about her the way other grown-ups had over the past year when they thought she wasn't in earshot: that for a young girl she was so silent and serious and grown-up. (Among other discomforts that year, she'd experienced a growth spurt: six inches taller, breasts and a period—a sudden possession by an awkward, alien body.)

Most of the books and newspaper clippings and ephemera unearthed by the diligent librarian contained little more than the story she'd heard from the woman by the lake. But she read it all, searching for a clue. In old newspapers, she learned of births and weddings and deaths. As the days went on she began to feel she knew the citizens of Hekate. Rebecca Wall, who'd given birth to triplets; Richard Hudson, who shot his father dead in an argument; Old Thomas Elbert, who fell asleep by the fire and burned his feet off. Likely, the newspaper regretted, "he would never recover from his injuries." There had been some sort of slave uprising, and there were references to terrible atrocities, but some editions of the paper were missing and so Ellen found it hard to follow the story.

In her third week of investigating, she came across an illustration in a book unreliably titled *Moonshine: Tales of Southern Haints, Hags, and Harrowing Happenings*. The illustration was much like those in the lake woman's book, a drawing of an unremarkable mid-nineteenth century Southern town, but several paragraphs drew her attention.

As the town of Hekate sank into decline, it became known locally as "the witch-town", and was said to have fallen under the influence of a sorceress. A number of slaves fled the area, unpursued by their owners, as the town increasingly isolated itself. Arriving in the North as free men, the former slaves spoke of arcane rites and rituals and sacrifices, but these reports were dismissed as superstition.

In time, however, more stories surfaced, including rumours that the town practiced a dangerous and degraded form of an ancient religion imported by its founder. As the town's reputation diminished, fewer and fewer tradesmen visited, and after the Civil War, it sheltered a few soldiers who had limped home from the battlefields, starving and diseased. Those they met on their long march back spoke of men in the grip of a delirium—remarkable even amid the suffering and devastation of the defeated armies—of eyes that shone unnaturally bright, and of disturbing, incoherent speech.

Locals avoided the town after its demise, citing an unwholesome atmosphere about the entire area.

Ellen checked the book out of the library and took it home, where she googled Hekate: a goddess of the underworld, she read, of sorcery, of magic, of boundaries between worlds. The red mullet was sacred to Hekate, and Ellen remembered the red fishes swarming around them in the underwater city.

She also found the red-haired woman on the website for the University of Georgia history department. Dr. Elizabeth Price was on sabbatical, the faculty page informed her. Ellen wasn't sure what a sabbatical was, but she clicked on the email link and started writing to her: We met last summer. You told me. My sister. Her words seemed inadequate and confused, and in the end she deleted it all. She went to close the email window but pressed "send" by accident; moments later an auto-reply lodged in her inbox informing her that Dr. Price would not return until the following January.

Of course there wouldn't be anyone she could tell her story to. What would this woman have thought, to receive such a rambling and fantastical tale?

At night the lost town of Hekate infected Ellen's dreams. In the dreams she was forever searching for Josie in the schools of reddish fish, through doorways leading nowhere, and roads that vanished into water and silt.

Summer drew to its end, and still she dreamed. They received their first letter from Cole since basic, a bleak note all the grimmer for its effort to sound cheerful. He enclosed a photo of himself, smiling without a hint of happiness under an unforgiving desert sun, and something gone from his eyes reminded Ellen of Josie. And then autumn closed in.

Ellen had started the school year off badly; for the first time ever, her parents had been called in for a special conference in those early weeks. She'd been such a good student, they were told. She'd done so well last year, in the wake of what happened. Now she was surly, unresponsive, hadn't turned in any work at all. Hadn't turned in any work? Ellen's mother looked at her, slumped miserably in her chair—*What are you doing then? What are you writing in your notebooks every night? I thought you were doing schoolwork.*

At home, they confiscated her notebooks, and found Ellen's work of the past weeks: endless drawings of a nineteenth-century town, from street scenes and maps to floor plans of buildings, and page after page of unreadable writing. Her mother shook the notebooks at her. *What is this? What's wrong with you?* Ellen couldn't say; she didn't know herself, and she'd long since passed through the fear they were just beginning to feel, and into a kind of acceptance.

The school was confounded. Her parents were confounded. No one knew what to do with her. Ellen felt like the eye of the storm. She watched and waited.

She woke early on the anniversary of Josie's disappearance. Beth still breathed regularly in the other bed—she'd never been sleepless in her life. Ellen dressed quietly and slipped out before anyone woke up.

It was a mile's hike to the highway, and she didn't have to wait long with her thumb out before a truck slowed and came to a stop. The driver was fat and kind-faced, and around her father's age; he had a cross dangling from the rear-view mirror and a Bible in the well between the seats. "Not used to seeing a young lady hitching by herself," he said. "You need to be careful." For once Ellen was grateful for the ungainly height that disguised just how young she was.

He drove her all the way out to Sorrow Lake and regarded her with concern as she stepped out of his cab. "Here," he said, holding out two twenties from his wallet. "Get yourself back home again."

Ellen shook her head. "I'm not going home," she said, though she had no idea what she'd really do, but he pressed the money on her anyway. She felt his eyes still on her as she crossed the parking lot and the artificial beach, heard him turn the rig around and leave.

She lowered herself to the sand, near where she'd sat the previous year, waiting for Josie to resurface. Maybe she could make it happen now. Maybe if she squeezed her eyes shut and made her thoughts very still, she could go back to that morning, she could go back before that, she could wake up when Josie slipped out of the cabin, and stop her doing whatever it was she had done.

Whatever it was she had done . . .

Ellen opened her eyes again. For a whole year, she'd believed that she'd failed Josie, that Josie had brought her out to the lake as a kind of talisman, to keep herself grounded. For an entire year, she'd believed that her sister had turned to her for help and she had been found wanting.

Now she understood.

The sibilant voices she'd strained so hard to hear were rising, only this time she could make out bits of what they were saying, and they called out to her; they sang of the path to the city, and she could see the schools of fish assembling, waiting to guide her down the silt roads to the deepest depths.

Josie had brought her baby sister along not for protection, but as a companion. Until Josie went away to Iraq, the two of them had scarcely been apart, and now they needn't be separated any longer.

Ellen got to her feet, and the trucker's money fluttered from her hands. The lake glistened red with fish, hundreds of them, just below the surface. She waded in, the water sloshing her jeans, past her ankles to her knees.

And she knew moments of hesitation then, with the air so pure and cool, the tentative morning sun on her arms, visions of herself growing up, growing older, of all the grief and all the sweetness ahead of her that would never come to pass. A few fish darted forward, sensing her indecision, and she backed away. The fish followed her as far as they could, their sucking mouths rising to the surface to gasp at the air, helpless to reach her.

She knew she should retreat to the safety of the parking lot, and the road beyond, but instead she walked along the curve of the lake and into the wood towards Uncle Hugh's cabin. She wasn't ready to face the questions, the anger and confusion of her family. She knew, though, that she didn't want to follow Josie, and all the others who had gone before. She wanted to grow up, and go away, and do all the foolish and unexpected and wonderful things that people do in the course of their lives.

They were calling again, their voices soft and unyielding, calling her down and away. *Just one look.* She picked her way to the edge of the lake. The surface was smooth, blameless and bland. The fish had deserted her.

Her jeans were wet to the thighs; she felt encased in the flesh of something already dead.

And then a breeze stirred the surface of the lake, and the ruins of Hekate appeared, rippling along a black ribbon of road, shining dark beneath the waters, the vision that had consumed her that whole long year.

The wind shifted, erasing the vision. Something told her this was her last chance. She might return to Sorrow Lake, but nothing would ever be the same.

One final look. She might find Josie down there. She might bring her back.

The soles of her shoes smacked the water, and with a sharp shock of cold the lake closed over her head. Fish surged round her, scales against flesh, tangling in her hair, drawing her into the wet rushing dark. Her shoes and jeans were heavy. The weight of the water crushed her memory of breath and light. Her descent swallowed time; seconds or aeons might have passed.

Blackness suffused her eyes and her ears and her nose. And then something glowed, not light, but a blacker blackness, a darkness so profound and alien it illuminated the sunken town, no longer a ruin, but restored. Blackness shone out from the highest spire, the church steeple, intricately twisted upon itself, knotted into nameless shapes that ought not to exist, beautiful and monstrous. Voices swelled from within the church itself, tones unheard in any register, rising to enmesh her. She kicked at the water and at the swarms of escorting fish, propelling her arms in an effort to thrust herself back towards the surface. She had seen enough. But Josie's name left her lips and was lost, and the singing engulfed her, and she plunged into the dark heart of Hekate.

The Haunting House

This. This house. This door, that sticks on opening. This worn old red stair runner, and the softness of a banister smoothed by generations of hands. This old clock on the landing, this little window, this turn in the stairs as they double back on themselves. This, the second storey, the narrow hallways and the friendly heavy cream-coloured doors with cosy rooms on the other side of them. Bedrooms with fireplaces! In childhood such a thing had seemed remarkable to her, and that had not changed. Lucy set down her bag, let its strap slip from her hand. She wanted to lie down right there and then on those cool floors, on those soft carpets, in front of that warm fire. She could feel the house embracing her as it always did, as it always had, as it always would. She was feeling so heavy and sleepy and peaceful.

Except for the buzzing sound. The buzzing grew louder and louder until it tore her from the cream-coloured door she was reaching out to open and deposited her in her own bed, or the bed that came with the room she was subletting at any rate, far from that safe warm house, with a relentless alarm rousing her to meet another pointless day.

It was seven days until Christmas, and she was utterly alone in the world.

She snatched her uniform from the night before off the hook on the back of her door and dressed quickly, grabbed her nametag off the bureau, shrugged into her coat, and ran down the stairs and out the door into a slushy and bleak Pacific Northwest winter afternoon. Late again: the bus just pulling away from the stop, ignoring her hailing hand. She started to walk, a fast walk in the rain, sweating in her coat inside the polyester uniform, another bus and another stop but this time she was going to have to wait; her alternate bus choice wasn't due for fifteen minutes. She could walk back to the previous stop, but in the time it would take, she'd probably miss that bus again as well. She pulled out her phone, stared at it, imagined the call she needed to make to her manager to explain she was going to be late yet again and just how well that was likely to go. Was it really necessary to trek all the way into work so that someone could fire you? Lucy put the phone away, trudged back up to the house that was not a home and the room that was not hers, undressed and went back into bed in hopes of recapturing the interrupted dream.

But this time her dreams were fitful and fretful; feverish, even. Tossing and turning, it was the buzzing of the phone that woke her this time—how much later? Hours? A day? And Meg's not-unexpected voice at the other end of it. Where the hell was she. Who the hell did she think she was. This was the last straw, did she understand that? She, Meg, had given her a chance, and then a lot more chances, and all she, Lucy, did with those chances was throw them back into people's faces. She, Meg, knew it was the holidays and all, but she had a restaurant to run, too, and Lucy couldn't keep on doing this to her and the rest of the staff.

You could only feel sorry for a person for so long before you realised there was a reason they were so far down on their luck, before you understood that it wasn't so much that life kept kicking them in the teeth as it was that they kept fucking over other people.

Lucy looked at her screen, let her thumb brush over the red icon there, and Meg's voice ceased. She stared at the screen for a few more moments till it vibrated to life with more angry buzzing. Meg again. She hit dismiss, then block.

Just like that, you slipped out of people's lives forever. It was the easiest thing in the world, once you got started.

First things first: sleep, a blessed thing. It was funny, she thought later, the way people talked about sleeping well. They speak of it in terms of things that don't sleep well at all. *I slept like the dead*, they say; *I slept like a baby*. Lucy slept like neither of those things. She slept like a very tired person, like a girl who had been holding onto too many things for too long and had suddenly let go of all of them at once, like a girl who had forgotten the miracle of sleep as a featureless void, a lost place where you could wander for hours unfettered by the cares of the world. She slept, and she slept, and she woke a little, only to do that most wonderful of things: remember that there was nothing that she had to get up for, and sink deeper into the bed, deeper into sleep.

In that time, she did not dream once of the house, or if she did, she did not remember it, and if she did not remember it, it had not been a real dream of the house: it had been some phantasm, some part of her brain mimicking the real dream.

She knew it was the kind of thing that explained to anyone would sound absurd, but that did not matter; she was not going to explain it to anyone, and she knew the difference between the real dream and the dream that was not real.

When she woke at last, she knew without checking that it was the next day, which meant that it was six days until Christmas. She lay for some time with heavy relaxed limbs and a head still dopey with sleep and considered her alternatives. This was something she had grown very skilled at doing, and she had learned a few things along the way. Mainly she had learned that as your existing alternatives shrank, considering them all became a much easier task.

Someone had said to her once that she was a passive person, that she waited for things to happen to her rather than making them happen herself. Or that when she did make things happen, she did so by forcing another person's hand, making them do the awful and unforgivable thing, burn the bridge between them from a sense of self-preservation. Lucy had thought that it was a cruel thing to say, but that did not mean that it was not also accurate.

So, losing another job: it was true that she'd forced her manager to fire her rather than quitting, but it had all been more deliberate than was usual for her all the same. She felt determined and clear-headed. She did not really need to consider her alternatives because she already knew which one she was going to choose.

You always heard about haunted houses. You never heard about someone who was haunted by a house. It was enough to make you wonder: all these years, had she stalked its corridors, terrifying its residents who were all unseen to her? Not once in her life had Lucy ever encountered another soul—another *living* soul, she'd nearly said to herself—in the house, but that had not seemed strange to her. She had always felt utterly complete in herself when she was there. She tried to imagine people there, but she could not. The house had clearly always been lived in and loved, but whoever lived there and loved it remained unseen.

She'd done a ghastly stint in therapy once, on the well-meaning advice of another someone, and she couldn't fault anyone for the awfulness of it, the therapist least of all, but it had been one of the most excruciating experiences of her short twenty-five years. She had gone in with all sincerity—it was one thing people often did not understand about Lucy, that she meant well, that she entered every situation with the intention of making the best of things—but it had been bad from the start. Because she had nothing really to say she'd made the mistake of bringing up the house—it seemed like the most interesting thing they could discuss, and the sort of thing therapists liked.

She had been too right. The therapist, clearly also sensing they had little to talk about, had pounced upon it. Her eagerness had been relentless. She had asked Lucy to describe all the rooms, to tell her everything she could remember about this lifelong recurring dream. She had wanted to know was there an attic and a basement, and if so what were they like, and was it big or small, and how were the rooms, and how did it all make her feel? As she peppered Lucy with questions, Lucy found herself lying; she felt pummelled by this kind grey-haired lady with a gentle voice who clearly wanted only to help her, only the problem was Lucy didn't *want* any help, she didn't *need* any help—well, scratch that, help was one thing she did need, but not of this sort. What was that saying? God helps those who help themselves. Well, there was no god, so clearly if there was any helping to be done it was going to come from her.

That had been a few years ago, and she had not yet been ready to help herself. On this unusually bright December morning, with six days left until Christmas, she thought this seemed as good a time as any to start.

Because the stint with the therapist had been about as useless as anything could possibly be, save for one aspect: she had come away from their sessions with the absolute conviction that the house was anything but a figment of her imagination, an expression of her subconscious, even a repressed memory or some past-life intrusion on the present.

The house was real.

Six days ticked down from five to four to three . . .

It was amazing how much free time you gained when you didn't have a job to go to. For at least another day or so Lucy found herself shocked into complacency at the slow passage of hours, of all the space that she had to move about in from waking to sleeping.

This had its disadvantages, like the fact that there were other people in the shared house whom she'd rarely seen when she was working odd hours all the time, but now she encountered them in awkward places: going into the kitchen, or walking out of the bathroom, or on the stairs. She'd never had much of a head for people, and the residents of the house confused her: she could never remember how many there were and sometimes she forgot their names, and it didn't help that they seemed equally disconcerted by her presence. She was subletting, ostensibly for two more months, from a girl named Shawna who'd gone somewhere (India?) and left all her belongings behind in a rather cluttered bedroom that meant a shockingly cheap rent that was just right for someone like Lucy, the type of someone who drifted here and there and had accumulated precious few things of her own. But in exchange for a few bits of furniture and a cheap rent she found herself, waking each morning as she did surrounded by someone else's things, forgetting who she was. On occasion she even woke and thought *my name is Shawna*, but the house usually stepped in and helped her out—*the* house, that is, not the house she was currently living in but the only house that mattered. When she became confused, the house reminded her with gentle nudges that she was Lucy, and it revealed to her again its warm corridors and inviting rooms, and she would settle gently back into herself again.

Another disconcerting aspect of the endless swathes of time she now had before her was her increased awareness of the preparation for Christmas. Some of the people in the house were going away and some were not, but until then someone had hung a wreath on the front door, and sometimes there was jolly Christmas music coming from someone's room. One evening most of the household had piled into the living room to watch old Christmas specials on DVD. She tried to participate, she really had, and it wasn't that she didn't remember the images flickering there from her own childhood, the stop-motion puppets, the strange anthropomorphic animal stories about mice and bears and other creatures who all seemed intent on celebrating the holiday as well. It was that she watched them across a great gulf the others did not seem to feel.

She was haunted, and always had been; they were not. It was as simple as that.

This. This house. This door—it does not stick this time, someone has seen to it, oiled it or seasoned it or sanded it down. The worn old stair runner is still here, as is the bannister, oiled and fresh and soft from generations of palms sliding along its length. Here, the friendly face of the grandfather clock on the landing, *tick, tick, tick*, and a turn in the stairs, now doubling back and up to the second storey. The hallways are narrow but they feel cosy, not cramped, and she can hardly wait to push open one of the doors and settle into the room on the other side, to light the fire that she knows has already been laid in preparation for her arrival. She knows that the bed will be turned back, and although the room will have an edge of chill on it at first, it will quickly dissipate. She knows it is going to feel like home. She sets down her bag, lets its strap slip from her hand and—

Something is wrong.

Her mind is racing, a thing it has never had to do before while in the house. It is turning over every step and every moment up to this one; it is desperate to detect what is off in this scenario. She is entirely certain that this is the real dream, so it isn't that. Was it the door that did not stick, the third step from the landing that did not gently give and groan in protest as her foot pressed into it? No, these were things that come and go. But she knew, then; the landing was the clue, for it was there she had turned, turned naturally to go up the next flight of steps and there *it* was—something that had scrambled out of sight so quickly that it did not register in her conscious mind at the time. Something pale and thin; she might have called it a ghost, but now that she was remembering it properly it had seemed horribly corporeal.

She woke this time with a gasp, eyes flashing open to unrelieved dark, hand skittering for the lamp, Shawna's lamp, next to the bed, and quick panicked thoughts as her eyes darted about the room: *I am in Shawna's room, I am Shawna*; but no, she was awake, and she was Lucy, and it was three days until Christmas, and she was haunted.

She got up from the strange bed that was not hers, went down to the strange kitchen that belonged to other people, and made herself a cup of herbal tea. It wasn't her tea either, but the girl it belonged to had a nice smile and always said she should help herself. Lucy never helped herself, and the girl, whose name she thought was Jenna, seemed almost affronted by this fact. So now Lucy would help others and help herself by way of a cup of Red Zinger tea, which on brewing did not taste nearly as evocative as the package had promised her it would.

After that there was no sleep for her. In fact, she was hesitant to even return to the room, even though it was nothing like the room in the dream, nor was the house. This was a modern split-level suburban-style house, not so different if much shabbier from the one she had grown up in; its sin was ugliness but not ghosts.

Still, for the first time ever, the dream had left her shaken, and here in the kitchen she felt safer than in Shawna's room. She waited until dawn and then she decided that was enough waiting, and then she called her mother.

At any rate, she tried to. A woman with a thick Spanish accent answered the phone and explained to her that no, her mother was away for the next few weeks. On a cruise, it sounded like, although Lucy hadn't known cruises lasted that long. Probably something was getting lost in translation. They ended up confusing one another equally; when Lucy explained that she had just been hoping to speak to her mother, the woman fell silent, and Lucy guessed either the woman hadn't heard of her or she had, and either way that was bad news, because Lucy hadn't spoken to her mother in more than six years. She came from a rich, unpleasant family and she couldn't deny that this had made her more irresponsible than most; always in the back of her mind was the knowledge that someone would probably bail her out in a pinch. Only here was the pinch, and here was the someone, only there was no one. Her mother, off in god-knew-where, with god-knew-whom, doing god-knew-what.

I don't believe in god, Lucy reminded herself, and as she set the phone down thought it was just as well. She thought about phoning her brother, but speaking of bridges and burning, that was one she wasn't willing to cross. He was more unpleasant than the whole lot of the rest of them put together, and that was saying something.

She *was* on her own then. She fixed herself another cup of Red Zinger and weighed her options once more. Because she was turning over a new leaf, she would not take the easy way out and walk out on the two months' rent the absent Shawna and the others in the house would be expecting, but this new leaf was going to cost her most of what she had left sitting in her bank account. That meant that if she was going to find the haunting house, she needed to be clever about it. It wasn't as though she had the resources to go traipsing all over the country and maybe even the world in search of a place she had only dreamed about.

There was also the matter of the pale corporeal thing on the landing, and that made her felt small and sick and scared. But if the thing was there, she must confront it as well.

That evening one of the residents of the shared house, a tall hipster type named Ambrose with a big mountain-man beard, brought home an enormous Christmas tree. It was so large they had to lop off the top to get it into the house. Finally they managed, but there was no tree stand, so they leaned it up against the wall and looked puzzled as it slowly dawned on them that they had no decorations either. Lucy watched most of these proceedings from her usual distant vantage point, but they all seemed so helpless regarding the tree stand and the lack of decorations that she took the bus to a Wal-Mart and picked one up, along with boxes of tinsel and lights and little gold and blue baubles. When she struggled home through the door overburdened with the packages you would have thought she was Santa

Claus himself, but even as the others were exclaiming over her purchases and the unexpected generosity from their normally reclusive housemate, she realised that once again this new leaf of hers had consequences. Her purchases had cost her exactly fifty-eight dollars and thirty-nine cents, and given that she had two months' rent to pay, no job, and a haunting house to find, presenting the others with a Christmas miracle wasn't the wisest allocation of funds. She thought again, briefly, about phoning the terrible brother— but no. She would manage. She always did.

This house. This door, that no longer sticks because maybe it is not the same door, maybe it is never the same door, maybe they have switched the doors on her and other things as well. This worn old red stair runner, gaping holes in it where it's worn down to the wood beneath. This banister that could trick you, not so sturdy, so that when you snatch at it as you might do if the worn runner catches your heel and pitches you forward, it might betray you, its smooth surface giving you no purchase as you tumble down, down—

But you are not tumbling down. You are continuing up. The grandfather clock on the landing, stern and disapproving, and a little window that shows you a world outside you can never be a part of. The turn in the stairs, the narrow hallway, the doors a sickly yellow—what is on the other side of them? What can be? Lucy set her bag down gingerly, quietly, so as not to let anyone know she was there. She fought the sleep that the house used to claim her. The fatigue pressed on her until she couldn't breathe, and she fought to get free of it, from a sudden sense that she had been buried alive, that she must dig out of her own grave, and she thrust off the covers and sat gasping, drenched in sweat, fumbling for the light to bring herself back to Shawna's bed, Shawna's room, and it was two days until Christmas. She had better get a move on if she was going to find the house in time.

Lucy had had no one to Christmas shop for since she was a teenager. Then it had been fun, out in the cold with friends, sometimes with snowflakes landing and melting on their coats and mittened hands. Then, the house had seemed like an extra charm in her charmed life, a lovely dream of a place she imagined she might live in someday. It was easy, then, to be a girl who was smart and rich and pretty, or so she told herself. She had to because otherwise she had to tell herself the truth: that nothing was as easy as it ought to be, that her family didn't love her or one another, that she wasn't sure she liked herself all that much.

Nearly a decade later here she was, not Christmas shopping, wading through a crunch of shoppers past Pioneer Square downtown, someone that was maybe Bing Crosby singing about a sleigh ride from a nearby shop, all of it aggressively cheerful. She tried to remember when she had started hating Christmas and then wondered when she had ever loved it.

She remained uncertain as to what exactly she was doing. She had packed a bag; she was headed for the bus station, but how could she purchase a ticket if she did not know the destination? Anyway, the thought of icy Oregon roads vanishing into winter landscapes frightened her. Most of the population clung to the upper northwest corner of the state, with the rest scattered down the west side of the Cascades; go east and she'd be headed into its remote heart and its eastern edges where high desert country met stark mountain ranges and the scope of the landscape made people seem puny and small.

All the same, at the bus station she named a destination; she did not think she had ever heard of the place, but it rolled easily off her tongue. Then she asked the man in the ticket booth to show her on the map where she was going. He pointed to a place somewhere in the eastern part of the state that truly looked like the middle of nowhere. There was a road, but only just, and in those areas what a map reported as a road might be little more than a dirt track. It was a request stop, he said. Be sure the bus driver knew that she needed to get off there or there was no telling where she might end up.

This house, this door, these steps, this carpet, this banister. There is a hole in the roof of this house and it is snowing inside and it is rotting the steps so they are unsafe to ascend. Lucy took them gingerly, testing her weight each time, but as she went higher they grew icy and the climb became more perilous. Here, at last, the relief of the landing, but the grandfather clock is clanging and it will not stop, chiming out all the hours at the same time, as though it is shouting at her. Turn round and up the next flight but this is where she stops altogether. The second storey, the narrow hallway, the shut-off rooms await her but she cannot make herself draw closer. She stops, three steps from the passageway above. Her bag slips from her hand and tumbles down the stairs, never to be seen again. She cannot go up or down. She is trapped forever on this staircase in the cold in this house.

Lucy woke with a start, and as she did, she so disturbed the person sitting next to her that they got up and moved away from her. Then as she came fully awake she stretched out a hand to the vinyl seat beside her and felt how cold it was; no one had been sitting beside her. In fact, the bus was nearly empty. There was someone at the back, but she had not caught a glimpse of their face.

She remembered what the ticket man had said about the request stop, and she panicked that she had missed it, so she made her way swaying to the front of the bus and asked the driver. He nodded. "Just up ahead," he said, "I won't forget about you," and then glanced back at her. She wanted to tell him to keep his eyes on the road, where snow swirled in the black night.

"Your people meeting you there?" he asked. "It's not a night for a young lady to be out in. Or anybody for that matter. Especially on Christmas Eve."

"Christmas Eve is tomorrow," she said.

"Not any more. It's past midnight."

She said, "I'm meeting people. And going to a place." It sounded false even to her, but he seemed satisfied enough. As she continued to stand there in the aisle, he asked, "Was there something else you needed?" and she said, "Oh! Sorry!" and headed back to her seat. A moment later though she remembered that she did have a question, and she made her way back to the front. "Excuse me," she said. "Sorry to bother you again, but I wanted to ask you about the other person on the bus."

"The other person?"

"Yeah, or the other two, I guess? One in the back and someone was sitting next to me a little while ago, I think."

"Couple folks got off way back in Eugene. That was hours ago. You're my only passenger. They didn't go off and leave you, did they?"

She looked to the back of the bus, sure that he was wrong, but saw no one. A terrible image entered her mind:

someone crawling, slowly and silently up the aisle, someone who did not want to be seen.

"No," she said. She tried desperately to think of another question to ask him so that she would not have to return to her seat, but he was easing over to the side of the road now. Alarmed, imagining something was wrong with the bus, she said, "What's wrong?"

He glanced back at her again. "This is your stop, isn't it? Didn't you say somebody would be here to meet you?" He peered out into the swirling snow. "I don't see anyone."

"No." She was talking too fast and too loud, moving back up the aisle to grab her bag from her seat and back again. "No, it's fine, I know where to go. Thank you."

"I've got a schedule to keep so I can't wait around," he said dubiously. "Sure you don't want to just stay on till we get someplace more populated? I won't charge you extra for it."

"No, no," and a nervous laugh escaped her. "This is where I need to get off." She was pressing up against the doors of the bus like he wasn't going to let her out, and then nearly tumbled into the snow when he did open them.

Just as he eased them shut she felt it: something that slipped off the bus behind her.

She whirled round to stop the driver, to say there had been someone, to implore him not to leave her here with some crazy person from the Greyhound, but there was no one there.

Worse, really, there was no one *here* either: she had followed a whim to the middle of nowhere. She flashed, for one moment, on Shawna's room back in the house in Portland. The house was probably empty now, everyone gone somewhere for Christmas while she had nowhere to go.

That was untrue. She *did* have somewhere to go, more than anyone perhaps.

Lucy shouldered her bag and began trudging through the snow, up the road.

This. This house.

She could scarcely believe her eyes, although of course it was what she had come here to find, and had it not been here, she did not know what she would have done.

It was just off the road, up a shortish drive. No vehicles parked in front to indicate anyone lived there, but its windows were ablaze with light.

She made her way slowly up the driveway. There was the door, just as it had always been in her dream. Would it stick?

She thought that in the nearly seven years since she had estranged herself from her family, she had been working her way here, across the country to this place.

She moved closer. Her hand on the doorknob. The door did not stick. In fact, it swung open so readily she half-expected someone to be on the other side of it. The only reason she knew someone was not was because there never had been, in her dreams.

She stepped across the threshold. Someone had been decorating for Christmas; not visibly, where she stood in the foyer, but she could smell the pine scent of the tree, and the warm smell of spices like cinnamon and nutmeg.

Here was the worn red carpet. It was not dirty, and the stairs were not broken, and the banister was not shabby. It was the house of her dreams, the right dreams, and here was the friendly grandfather clock, its low tone chiming the hour.

Nearly two a.m. She must get to bed soon.

Outside the little window on the landing, the snow was falling harder.

Now up the second flight. She had dreamed of this so many times, and each time it had been so real, but never like this. There was still dream-real and real-real, and she knew which one this was. She knew there was no waking from *this*, not in Shawna's room or anywhere else.

The narrow hallway. The bedroom doors, all in warm cream colours. She was so tired and achy, and she thought of the fire she would light and the heavy blankets on the bed that she would sink into. She would be warm and safe.

A creak on the stairs behind her startled her. She swung round. There was nothing behind her, or not that she could see, but as she turned and turned again, she had the sensation of something turning along with her, yet always just behind her.

She asked the house a question: "How can you be? Why are you here?"

Not every house has to occupy a particular place, does it? Perhaps she had not been moving toward the house; perhaps the house had been moving *with* her, from her New England home to the South, to the Midwest, and across the country to this remote Oregon landscape where everything was a million miles from everything else. She thought that if she were to leave it now, to try to trek back to the road where the bus had left her, she would not find any of it, and indeed she knew without looking that the snowdrifts must be piled high already.

She knew now how the house would appear from the outside. Had the bus driver seen the derelict structure she had come such a long way to spend the night in he would not have allowed her off the bus; he would not have even stopped. He'd have driven on through the night as fast as he safely could.

She retraced her steps back down: here the worn red runner, ragged with mildew; here the grandfather clock, smashed by vandals decades ago; the turn here on the stairs, stairs which surely must be unsafe, stairs that ought not to bear her weight but they bore her because the house bore her, because the house loved her. The door swung open and shut, open and shut, because the catch was broken, and snow and the wind were blowing in.

This she knew: that at last she was loved. And the house had loved others. She could sense them even if she could not yet see them. But it loved her, Lucy, best of all, that much she was sure of. And she loved it back. She told it so, and the broken bones of its structure, the rotting heart of its foundation, embraced her. The others were not far behind.

It was almost Christmas, and Lucy belonged somewhere at last.

For Sean

Story Notes

Where do stories come from? The first one in this collection, "The Receiver of Tales", attempts to grapple with this question. These stories come from all over the place—incidents from my life, scraps of conversation I overhear, things I read, the inside of my own head. But for as much as I tend to fold bits of autobiography into fiction, they are rarely the identifiable bits, and anyway things change so much in service to the narrative that sometimes they rarely resemble what they began as. Below are some notes about how the stories in *You'll Know When You Get There* began their lives and how the act of making them into fiction changed them.

"The Receiver of Tales"

I wrote the opening of this story a long time ago. I really did get to know a next-door neighbour once when he slipped a painting under my door because he wanted "to meet the girl who plays the Pixies all the time". I didn't know where to go with the story after that, but I knew it was an opening that would become something eventually. Years later, Kate Jonez asked me to write a story around the idea of a compulsion. I was originally going to write something around the idea of a person's compulsive relationship with their past, but somehow it turned into a story *about* storytelling. I think we all—writers and non-writers alike—have a compulsion to some degree to tell stories and try to shape the absurd mess of our lives into something that resembles that sense of a narrative.

"Widdershins"

The idea for this story started with a friend's Facebook status update that is now echoed in the tale's opening lines. I thought it sounded unexpectedly sinister and wrote it down. I set the story primarily in a little village in a remote part of rural Ireland where I once lived for almost a year. When the story was in progress, I went to visit the friend who wrote the status update. We went for a long walk in the Wicklow countryside and found the famine cottages as well the stream. But we did not end up in the forest as in the story—I lived to tell the tale.

"The House on Cobb Street"

I've written elsewhere about hypnagogic hallucinations—to which I am not ordinarily prone—as one of the origins of this tale; I woke and heard little girls whispering. This was one of the those stories that flowed naturally, in that I didn't think about its epistolary form—it simply wanted to be told in that way from the start. As for the rest of it—I love haunted house stories, and I believe this may be the very first one I've ever written (but by no means the last, as evidenced by the other tales that appear in this volume.)

"Where the Summer Dwells"

This story has its genesis in a number of different places. A few years before actually writing it, I had watched the documentary *Searching for the Wrong-Eyed Jesus*. It's a film I love, but in many ways it's a very romantic evocation of the South. It's region as myth, and as a result it simultaneously feels both very spot-on and very removed from its actual subject, if such a thing is possible. Like Charlotte in the story, I did spend a summer with one of my best friends exploring all the broken-down houses and cemeteries and dirt roads in our rural county. I think this is a kind of love story to that region, about which I have all kinds of contradictory feelings; it's also something of a nod to the influence of Karl Edward Wagner, whose story "Where the Summer Ends" was also about the Southern landscape and, more specifically, the exceptionally creepy kudzu.

"Who Is This Who Is Coming?"

In the summer of 2015, I spent a weekend at the same place Fern does in this story, and as I was standing in the cemetery, the title, the character, even her name, Fern Blackwell, came to me unbidden, along with an image of the figure standing down by the shore. I didn't get a chance to visit all the places Fern does, but you can go to Happisburgh and stay in the signal box, and see the lighthouse and the churchyard—but I would be careful about where you walk at night, and to whom you speak, and I wouldn't go digging for ancient treasure on the beach.

"The Queen in the Yellow Wallpaper"

Titles are often the last thing that come to me, but this story started with the title, which sprung unbidden into my head and begged to have a story built around it. Like "The House on Cobb Street" and parts of "Where the Summer Dwells", the writing of this story had a feverish, compulsive quality to it, almost as though in places I were setting down a story I was being told rather than writing myself. It's one of my favourite stories I have written with one of my favourite opening lines.

"The Wife's Lament"

Years ago, as part of my work on a master's degree in medieval English literature, I did a translation of the Old English lyric "The Wife's Lament", and ever since, I have wanted to write a contemporary story around it. It's an absolutely fascinating piece, utterly enigmatic, and with a few translation-related ambiguities that make it both opaque and open to interpretation. I had several false starts and stops along the way before I found the right characters and situations, although I'm still not sure I've got the poem out of my system. I think there might be an entire novel lurking somewhere in those lines! The story's dedicated to my amazing professor and thesis advisor from those days, Christine Rose.

"This Time of Day, This Time of Year"

I grew up fascinated with stories of a sunken city near where I grew up in Petersburg, Georgia, and I had always wanted to write a story about it. Josie was a character I'd wanted to write about for a long time too. The plight of the returning soldier, the one who is unable to adjust to civilian life after such terror and adrenaline—and I think in some ways the euphoria of war—is another theme that has long fascinated me. It's a character type I identify with strongly—I suspect the sort of soldier I would be. I also wanted to write specifically about a woman who was in the military. This is the first kind of explicitly Lovecraft-inspired story I've ever written, although some people think the story "These Things We Have Always Known" from my first collection, is Lovecraftian. I think there's certainly arguably an element of that.

This story really only scratches the surface of a fascination I have with this particular type of character, and as with the poem "The Wife's Lament", I think I will be returning to her in the future.

"The Haunting House"

I wrote this story as a Christmas present for Sean Hogan in 2014, although its origins lie in a detour I once took in an Oregon desert. Being from the Southeast, I never adjusted to the scale of the landscape in the West and how remote and deadly it can be. I once turned off a main road onto what looked like a side road on the map, but actually turned out to be little more than a dirt footpath. I bumped along it for a few miles in the rental car until I came to an abandoned house. That's all, just the abandoned house. It gave me one of the most awful feelings, as though Leatherface or that creature from *Jeepers Creepers* was going to come running at me from around the corner. It was the house I had in mind when I started this story, but I'm not sure whether or not it's the same house Lucy wound up in at the end. Has she been taken in and embraced by something dreadful, something *not sane*, like Eleanor in *The Haunting of Hill House*, or does this collection actually end on a happy note? I'm going to leave that for you to decide.

Acknowledgements

Thanks to the editors who initially published these stories: Kate Jonez, Michael Kelly, John Joseph Adams, Gordon Van Gelder, Johnny Mains, David Longhorn, and Peter Crowther, and to Stephen Jones and Ellen Datlow for the reprints. Perpetual special thanks go to Andy Cox.

Years ago, Lisa Tuttle published a classic collection of short stories, *A Nest of Nightmares*, that was hugely influential for me. Having her agree to write the introduction to this collection is an enormous honour, and it's also a real thrill to think how excited my twenty-year-old self would have been if she could have looked into the future and seen this.

Thanks also go to Tobia Makover for making such wonderful art that so compellingly evokes moods similar to those I strive for in my fiction, and to Linette Dubois for introducing me to her work—and for decades of friendship! James Bacon set this collection in motion; Sean Hogan got to its essence and gave it a title. Finally, thank you to Jim Hinson for the author photograph; Ken Mackenzie, Jim Rockhill, and Meggan Kehrli for their patience; and, of course, Brian J. Showers, for the wonderful work on this book.

Sources

"The Receiver of Tales"
was first published in *Little Visible Delight*,
Omnium Gatherum Media, 2013.

"Widdershins" was first published in
Shadows & Tall Trees 5, Summer 2013.

"The House on Cobb Street" was first published in
Nightmare Magazine, June 2013.

"Where the Summer Dwells" was first published in
The Magazine of Fantasy & Science Fiction
September/October 2012.

"The Queen in the Yellow Wallpaper"
was first published in *The Burning Circus*,
British Fantasy Society, 2013.

"The Wife's Lament" was first published in
Supernatural Tales 24, August 2013.

"This Time of Day, This Time of Year"
was first published in *Postscripts 30/31*,
PS Publishing, August 2013.

"Who Is This Who Is Coming?"
and "The Haunting House"
appear here for the first time.

About the Author

Lynda E. Rucker is an American writer born and raised in the South and now living in Europe. Her stories have appeared in dozens of magazines and anthologies. She edited the anthology *Uncertainties III* for Swan River Press in 2018, had a short play produced on London's West End, and won the 2015 Shirley Jackson Award for Best Short Story. Her first collection, *The Moon Will Look Strange*, was published by Karōshi Books in 2013.

SWAN RIVER PRESS

Founded in 2003, Swan River Press is an independent
publishing company, based in Dublin, Ireland, dedicated
to gothic, supernatural, and fantastic literature. We special-
ise in limited edition hardbacks, publishing fiction from
around the world with an emphasis on Ireland's contribu-
tions to the genre.

www.swanriverpress.ie

*"Handsome, beautifully made volumes . . .
altogether irresistible."*

– Michael Dirda, *Washington Post*

*"It [is] often down to small, independent, specialist presses
to keep the candle of horror fiction flickering . . . "*

– Darryl Jones, *Irish Times*

*"Swan River Press has emerged as one of the most inspiring
new presses over the past decade. Not only are the books
beautifully presented and professionally produced, but they
aspire consistently to high literary quality and originality,
ranging from current writers of supernatural/weird fiction
to rare or forgotten works by departed authors."*

– Peter Bell, *Ghosts & Scholars*

GHOSTS

R. B. Russell

Ghosts contains R. B. Russell's debut publications, *Putting the Pieces in Place* and *Bloody Baudelaire*. Enigmatic and enticing, they combine a respect for the great tradition of supernatural fiction, with a chilling contemporary European resonance. With original and compelling narratives, Russell's stories offer the reader insights into the more hidden, often puzzling, impulses of human nature, with all its uncertainty and intrigue. There are few conventional shocks or horrors on display, but you are likely to come away with the feeling that there has been a subtle and unsettling shift in your understanding of the way things are. This book is a disquieting journey through twilight regions of love, loss, memory and ghosts. This volume contains "In Hiding", which was shortlisted for the 2010 World Fantasy Awards.

> *"Russell's stories are captivating for their depth of mystery and haunting melancholy."*

– Thomas Ligotti

> *"Russell deals in possibilities beyond the rational."*

– Rue Morgue

> *"Quiet horror told in an unassuming, polished narrative style."*

– Hellnotes

THE SEA CHANGE
& Other Stories

Helen Grant

In her first collection, award-winning author Helen Grant plumbs the depths of the uncanny: Ten fathoms down, where the light filtering through the salt water turns everything grey-green, something awaits unwary divers. A self-aggrandising art critic travelling in rural Slovakia finds love with a beauty half his age—and pays the price. In a small German town, a nocturnal visitor preys upon children; there is a way to keep it off—but the ritual must be perfect. A rock climber dares to scale a local crag with a diabolical reputation, and makes a shocking discovery at the top. In each of these seven tales, unpleasantries and grotesqueries abound—and Grant reminds us with each one that there can be fates even worse than death.

"A brilliant chronicler of the uncanny as only those who dwell in places of dripping, graylit beauty can be."

– Joyce Carol Oates

"Meticulously written and with carefully calculated chills."

– Black Static

THE ANNIVERSARY
OF NEVER

Joel Lane

Joel Lane's award-winning stories have been widely praised, notably by other masters of weird fiction such as M. John Harrison, Graham Joyce, and Ramsey Campbell. His tales also regularly appeared in the "best of" annual anthologies of Ellen Datlow, Karl Edward Wagner, and Stephen Jones. With this posthumous collection, Lane continues his unflinching exploration of the human condition. "*The Anniversary of Never* is a group of tales concerned with the theme of the afterlife," observed Lane, "and the idea that we may enter the afterlife before death, or find parts of it in our world." These stories of love and death will burrow deep into the reader's mind and impregnate it with a vision often as bleak as the night is black.

*"Melancholy and bleak, the weird, often dark stories
in this slim, beautiful volume are a fitting coda
to Lane's life and work."*

– Ellen Datlow

*"A liminal collection whose ghost like state almost mimics
that of much of the material contained within its pages."*

– Black Static

*"Rich and varied forms of darkness
illuminated by the author's wit and intelligence."*

– Supernatural Tales